MARROW AND BONE

WALTER KEMPOWSKI (1929–2007) was born in Hamburg.
During World War II, he was made to serve in a penalty unit
of the Hitler Youth due to his association with the rebellious
Swingjugend movement of jazz lovers, and he did not finish
high school. After the war he settled in West Germany. On
a 1948 visit to Rostock, his hometown, in East Germany,
Walter, his brother Robert, and their mother were arrested
for espionage; a Soviet military tribunal sentenced him to
twenty-five years in prison, of which he served eight at the
notorious "Yellow Misery" prison in Bautzen. In 1957 he
graduated from high school. His first success as an author
was the autobiographical novel *Tadellöser & Wolff* (1971),
part of his acclaimed German Chronicle series of novels.
In the 1980s he began work on an immense project, *Echo
Soundings*, gathering firsthand accounts, diaries, letters, and
memoirs of the Second World War, which he collated and
curated into ten volumes published over twenty years, and
which is considered a modern classic. His 2006 novel, *All for
Nothing*, was translated by Anthea Bell and is available from
NYRB Classics.

CHARLOTTE COLLINS studied English literature at
Cambridge and worked as an actor and radio journalist before
becoming a literary translator. In 2017 she was awarded the
Goethe-Institut's Helen and Kurt Wolff Translator's Prize
for her translation of Robert Seethaler's *A Whole Life*.

MARROW AND BONE

WALTER KEMPOWSKI

Translated from the German by
CHARLOTTE COLLINS

NEW YORK REVIEW BOOKS

New York

THIS IS A NEW YORK REVIEW BOOK
PUBLISHED BY THE NEW YORK REVIEW OF BOOKS
435 Hudson Street, New York, NY 10014
www.nyrb.com

Originally published in the German language in 1992 as *Mark und Bein*.

Library of Congress Cataloging-in-Publication Data
Names: Kempowski, Walter, author. | Collins, Charlotte, 1967– translator.
Title: Marrow and bone / by Walter Kempowski ; translated by Charlotte
  Collins.
Other titles: Mark und Bein. English
Description: New York : New York Review Books, 2020. | Series: New York
  Review Books classics | Translated from the German.
Identifiers: LCCN 2019027201 (print) | LCCN 2019027202 (ebook) |
  ISBN 9781681374352 (trade paperback) | ISBN 9781681374369 (ebook)
Classification: LCC PT2671.E43 M3713 2020 (print) | LCC PT2671.E43
  (ebook) | DDC 833/.914—dc23
LC record available at https://lccn.loc.gov/2019027201
LC ebook record available at https://lccn.loc.gov/2019027202

ISBN 978-1-68137-435-2
Available as an electronic book; ISBN 978-1-68137-436-9

Printed in the United States of America on acid-free paper.
10 9 8 7 6 5 4 3 2 1

For Robert

For the word of God is quick, and powerful, and sharper than any two-edged sword, piercing even to the dividing asunder of soul and spirit, and of the joints and marrow, and is a discerner of the thoughts and intents of the heart.

Hebrews 4:12

I

On Isestrasse in Hamburg there stands a row of imposing houses from the turn of the twentieth century. They tower behind ancient black chestnut trees, five or six storeys high, grandly built, adorned with stucco tendrils, their date displayed triumphantly on the gable. Decrepit lifts with wrought-iron grilles go up and down in their tiled stairwells. Juddering up and down in these lifts, you feel you could be in Paris – Paris, London or Milan.

Isestrasse would not have been left standing after the war if the bomb aimers of the Allied air forces had pressed their release buttons a hundredth of a second earlier or later. Firestorms all around, explosions, people buried alive – but Isestrasse did remain standing, and still stands today, with its tiled stairwells and antique lifts, in spite of property speculation and a mania for renovation.

The street is always bathed in the genteel shade of the huge chestnut trees, and every five minutes a train thunders along the steel girders of the elevated railway. Local antiques dealers would have robbed the girders of their art nouveau ornamentation long ago if such a thing were possible. Cars park under the railway, and a farmers' market is held there twice a week, selling pallid poultry, Black Forest stone-baked bread and unripe tropical fruit.

The railway runs in front of the houses, and behind them lies the Isebek canal, a murky, disused branch of the Alster on which tourists potter about in pedal boats.

In one of these houses lived Jonathan Fabrizius, known to his friends as 'Joe'. He was forty-three years old, of medium height, a man whose neatly parted blond hair was cut by a barber, not a stylist.

The best thing about him was his eyes. Neither short-sighted nor long-sighted, unimpeded by astigmatism, he registered all that he encountered. True, his ear lobes were always a little grubby, and he had been known to throw up in a wastepaper basket on occasion, but his eyes were bright and clear, and anyone who had anything to do with him was struck by them.

'Whatever he may be,' such people said, 'he's somehow . . . I don't know . . .'

Jonathan had studied a wide variety of things: German language and literature, history, psychology and art. He had climbed the rungs of the ladder, ascending ever higher, right up into the dusty rafters; he had gazed out through spider-blinded window slits across the verdant plain and been visited by clarity and truth. And now here he sat, with his clarity and truth, looking around him. What was he to do with all this refinement? What was it good for?

He was still enrolled at the university in order to keep his health insurance, but he had abandoned his studies. He earned a living writing newspaper articles and received regular commissions from journals and magazines because editors appreciated the verve of his diction and the punctuality of his delivery. He couldn't actually live on these commissions; he didn't have to, because he got a monthly allowance from his uncle, who owned a furniture factory in Bad Zwischenahn that manufactured in-expensive sofa beds of the simplest design for which there were always plenty of takers.

Jonathan occupied the room at the back of the apartment with a view of the Isebek canal. His girlfriend, Ulla, had the front room overlooking the street. The sliding door that linked the two large rooms – or separated them, depending on your point of view – was blocked off on Jonathan's side by a battered leather sofa and on Ulla's by bookshelves and a stereo that poured forth the familiar, old-fashioned melodies Ulla favoured, especially in the evenings: Mozart's Piano Concerto in E-flat major or the 'Prague' Symphony, with that squeak of the horn. Gilt-framed pencil sketches by Du Bois hung over her Biedermeier sofa, and a French lamp with an orange glass shade shed a cosy light on the coffee table.

Jonathan possessed neither a stereo nor a seating corner. The big leather sofa, sprouting horsehair from a rip in the seat, was his main item of furniture. This was where he slept, this was where he spilt his yoghurt and this was where he read a wide variety of popular scientific literature to maintain an overview, although he didn't really know to what end. The manual typewriter with its defective E sat in front of the sofa on a white kitchen table. Beside it were newspapers, books, a saucer full of matches, used earplugs and dirty socks. A naked lightbulb hung from a dusty stucco ceiling rose, and this gave enough light.

The parquet floor of his room was covered with linoleum. Jonathan had wanted to rip out this abstract-patterned floor covering because, he said, it prevented the wooden floor underneath from breathing. A large section had already been thrown out before his girlfriend discovered that the design on the flooring was an interesting piece of work from the early 1930s by Vladimir Kolaszewski, definitely worth preserving. Ever since, with its ruined flooring, his room had had a rather jerry-built appearance, as if there hadn't been enough money to finish the job. From time to time Jonathan would stare at the pattern on the linoleum, chewing his nails. He visualized it as a map, depicting roads, rivers and towns, and this served as a stimulus for long imaginative games. What a shame the piece he'd ripped out had been disposed of. He could have framed it and hung it on the wall.

Hanging there instead was a painting by Botero of a fat child in muted colours. Jonathan had acquired it in the 1960s and paid it off in hundred-mark instalments. From time to time the dealer he'd bought it from would ask him if he still wanted it. Wouldn't he like to sell it back to him?

All around the walls books were stacked untidily on the sticky floor, research for an extended feature on Brick Gothic architecture. He had rather lost sight of this undertaking; the magazine he had planned to write it for had not shown a great deal of interest. It was a southern German paper, the editors of which couldn't tell Stralsund from Wismar. They found the photos of the hulking great buildings rather off-putting: Kolberg, with that bulky, slanted roof? And a ruin as well?

Jonathan had a wardrobe containing some crumpled jackets; beside it was a makeshift washing area that could be divided off from the rest of the room by drawing a plastic curtain along a thin rod. When Jonathan washed his hands in the soap-encrusted basin he could see out of the window, and his glance would fall on a weeping willow trailing its branches in the murky water of the Isebek canal. No swans swam beneath it, but at least there were ducks.

The apartment's remaining rooms belonged to a general's widow. She was from the east, and seldom emerged from her dark vaults, where she relived memories of a bygone age. From time to time they heard her chesty cough, which she relieved by hawking into the kitchen sink.

Jonathan's girlfriend's full name was Ulla Bakkre de Vaera. She was dark-haired and of Swedish descent. She liked to wear a long knitted skirt with multicoloured horizontal stripes and a men's worsted jacket, shiny with wear, with a silver workman's watch in the breast pocket. Ulla had a pretty, round face still unmarked by the years: sweet at first glance, resolute at second. The thing that really bothered her was her left incisor. The nerve had been removed years ago and now the tooth was turning black, a blemish on her girlish features. Every morning she looked at this blemish in the mirror and was momentarily sad. Extraction or a crown? That was the question, and had been for years.

Ulla Bakkre de Vaera possessed a fine ring, a well-worn cameo on caramel-coloured stone that she had inherited from her father. It dated back to the second century BC, or so it had been claimed for generations, and ought really to have been handed down to a different branch of the family. It was thanks to this ring that she had got the part-time job at the municipal art museum; she was studying art history and financing her studies herself. Although the museum director had received a letter from her father intended to smooth her path, Dr Kranstöver had been on the verge of rejecting her as she sat there in his office – a tad too pretty, perhaps? But then his glance had fallen on the ring, and that had tipped the scales. Ulla got the job. She was allowed to show foreign guests around, edit catalogues and stand discreetly in a corner at exhibition openings, nodding at the director approvingly. One of these days he would take her out for a meal.

She had also been allowed to help design a children's corner in the museum, with tactile objects, squidgy carpets and the kind of slide they used to have in shoe shops. Children could draw on the walls with coloured chalk. Alas, these artworks could not be assimilated into the collection as the cleaning ladies rubbed them out every morning, shaking their heads.

Ulla was currently preparing an exhibition about depictions of cruelty in the visual arts. Her shelves were full of books showing all sorts of Inquisition torture, events from the Thirty Years War, and Goya, of course, his depictions of wartime atrocities. This was also where she kept her alphabetical card index, which comprised everything from disembowelling to the drawing of teeth. It was an anthology of cruelties that left no aspect of human fiendishness unexamined. And it wasn't all medieval panels. Every day the newspapers also provided material of interest: police in modern armour, blood-streaked victims of terrorism, South Africans with burning tyres about their necks. She must pay particular attention to the Africans, as an artistic rendering of this distinctive form of lynching was only to be expected.

None of these terrible images left the slightest impression on Ulla. As her studies had taught her, she considered only their formal aspects: the diagonals, for example, connecting extreme martyrdom with salvific objects, or the barely detectable way an artist had used light and shade to create emphasis, conveying a deeper meaning to the observer. The exhibition should not stimulate people's baser instincts; it should provoke revulsion, together with an energetic determination never to allow such things to happen again in this world. Evil exists in order to awaken good, which was why the exhibition catalogue would be prefaced by Mephistopheles' famous words from Goethe's *Faust*:

I am a part of that power which would
Do evil constantly, and constantly does good.

2

On a cool morning in August 1988 Jonathan sprang past the cleaning lady on his way up the stairs. He had been to the market to buy a bag of bread rolls and a bunch of flowers. As he hurried up, taking the stairs three at a time, he ran the forefinger of his left hand along the water lily tiles in the stairwell, holding the flowers and the bag of rolls in his right. The flowers were for Ulla, who turned twenty-nine today. She'd put up with him, as she expressed it, for three years now, although he thought he was actually the one who had put up with a lot.

Ulla was still in bed. She knew it was already nearly ten, and she'd realized that Jonathan had gone out for the rolls. She was still in bed because today that was her prerogative. She was thinking about a doll's house with a library and smoking room that she had seen in a shop on a nearby street: it could be destroyed at the touch of a button and was intended as a form of therapy through which children could channel their destructive urges. Ulla had always been interested in toys: figures with smoke cartridges at the back, wind-up animals that bared their teeth. People could buy little guillotines to celebrate the French Revolution. She could get hold of one and suggest it to the museum director as an exhibit.

*

Now Jonathan was banging about in the kitchen, and shortly afterwards he broke in on the muffled drowsiness of her doze, pulled aside the curtain with a clatter and sat down on the edge of her bed. Congratulations were in order. Jonathan got through the embarrassment of the little ceremony by uttering awkward clichés and stroking his girlfriend vaguely with his right hand, much as one might close the eyes of the dead, while simultaneously laying the breakfast table and setting out the boiled eggs with his left. He had to stand to light the candles and arrange the bunch of flowers, which brought the little ritual to an end.

He poured the coffee and shook the rolls out into the breadbasket. Then he extracted her birthday present from his wallet: a tiny Callot etching that depicted someone being sawn into pieces. He gave her the postage-stamp-sized etching and watched her closely to see what she would say about him giving her such a beautiful present. Bullseye! Ulla devoured the quartering with her eyes – 'Sweet!' – and leant it against the candlestick so she could look at it again and again. Then she drew her boyfriend down to her and gave him kisses like fiery little coins, holding his head in both hands as she did so.

When he was restored to freedom he took the post from his jacket pocket and sorted through it. Five letters were addressed to the birthday girl, two to him. She sat up, spread a roll with honey and read the letters, the contents of which were as you would expect.

Jonathan clumsily opened his two letters with his forefinger. One was from the Santubara car factory in Mutzbach – junk mail, presumably – the other from his Uncle Edwin in Bad Zwischenahn. It contained a cheque for more than two hundred marks and the suggestion that he do something sensible with it on this day.

'Treat yourselves to something,' his uncle wrote. 'Enjoy the good things in life.'

Conflicting emotions prevented Jonathan from showing the cheque to his girlfriend, who was busy with her own letters. He left it in the envelope and quickly slipped it into his pocket.

Ulla was from an orderly family; she had money in the bank and gilt-framed ancestral portraits. Jonathan, however, was born on a covered cart in East Prussia in February 1945, in an icy wind and sharp, freezing rain on the trek away from the Eastern Front. His young mother had 'breathed her last', as Jonathan put it, in the process. 'I never knew my parents,' he would say, usually with indifference. 'My father was killed on the Baltic coast, on the Vistula Spit, and my mother breathed her last after giving birth to me in East Prussia in 1945.' As far as suffering was concerned, this guaranteed him an unparalleled advantage over his friends.

That cold February, when calamity struck, his uncle had been driving the cart with its makeshift carpet roof, the pregnant woman tossing about inside the straw. When she went into labour he knocked on farmhouse doors to no avail, and so she died.

Her corpse had been set down quickly and without ceremony in the vestibule of a village church, beside the hymn board with its wooden numbers, and then they had driven on. They had come across a sturdy peasant woman who had lost her child, and she had nursed Jonathan in its place in return for a seat in the cart. Jonathan pictured this as well: the heavy woman sitting in the cart, with himself at her large breast, and the picture more or less corresponded to the reality.

I was suckled by Mother Earth, he would reflect on occasion, and he would stretch, feeling new strength in his veins.

Today Uncle Edwin had sent two hundred marks – the new Avanti sofa bed had been a hit.

Treat yourselves to something? That should be possible.

In the meantime Ulla had read her post: from her overbearing mother, her passive father, her psychologist brother in Berlin, and Evie, her goddaughter, whose birthday letter – 'how are you, I am fine' – was awkwardly written and decorated with ladybirds.

She got out of bed and went over to the bookshelf, where the present she had given herself was standing: a 1950s Danish vase, which the two of them now admired. It was held up to the light, turned this way and that and praised as 'frightful'. When they had finished with it they stood it on the window ledge alongside various other monstrosities, items that had once been dirt cheap but now had a certain value, or would have if left for a few more years.

Jonathan was embraced again, assured that his little Callot etching had been 'just right', and then dismissed. So he went back to his room, which he was happy to do, as the birthday girl was now making phone calls and he had no interest in one-sided conversations.

Jonathan sat down on his sofa. He blew some fluff from the table then stared off into the distance towards the bright window opposite and the portrait of the plump child on the grubby white wall.

He yawned, and his gaze drifted across the weird linoleum geography of his floor. He saw the Isthmus of Corinth, that hair-raising cleft in the rock; he saw a little ship, and steep rock walls to left and right. The water is flowing, he thought, and the ship glided down the canal as if caught in an undertow.

He snapped out of it and read the letter from the Santubara car manufacturer. As it turned out, it wasn't junk mail but a serious job offer. A Herr Wendland from the factory's press office wrote that they had been admirers of his discerning prose for quite a while now and were wondering whether Jonathan might fancy a trip to East Prussia; Masuria, to be precise, in present-day Poland. The Santubara Company wanted to set up a test-driving tour for motoring journalists to convince them of the outstanding quality of its latest eight-cylinder model. Any such tour would, of course, have to be carefully prepared in advance. Would Jonathan care to help with this? He could go along on the initial preparatory tour, check out the local culture, see whether there was anything worth visiting in the region – stately homes perhaps, or churches or castles the existence and histories of which might add something to the itinerary. Then he could write an insightful piece about the trip, say twelve pages of typescript – 'Masuria Today' – which they could use to convince journalists that it might be interesting to look around that godforsaken region and take the opportunity of test-driving the new eight-cylinder car at the same time. He would have completely free rein, and they could offer him five thousand marks plus expenses. Travel and accommodation would, of course, be included, so that would be five thousand plus VAT. The precise sum was negotiable.

Masuria? Poland?

Jonathan's first reaction was *no!* If it had been a trip through Spain or Sweden, then maybe. But Poland?

No.

On the other hand, five thousand marks . . . And negotiable?

Jonathan took down the 1961 edition of the *Iro World Atlas* – which he still used simply because that was the one he had – and opened it at the map of 'German Eastern Territories Under Foreign Administration'. Quite a sizeable chunk, East Prussia. How strange and unnatural the line was, drawn straight across it with a ruler. You saw that sort of thing on maps of colonial Africa or the Antarctic, but in the heart of Europe? It reminded Jonathan of dissection lines in pathology, scalpel incisions in a woman's flawless white body.

Here was the Vistula Spit, where his father was killed, and the Curonian Spit. Pictures from old geography books came to mind: wandering dunes, elk, a fisherman sitting on his upturned boat mending a net, amber mining.

But the plague arrived by the light of the moon,
Swam with the elk across the lagoon.

Jonathan looked for the village of Rosenau, tracing the road with his finger. Here: this was where it happened. This was where he had first seen the light of day, at the cost of his mother's life. Here, in this village church, was where she had been set down. The young woman had been buried in the churchyard, by the wall perhaps, beneath a laburnum. There was a single photograph of her still in existence, one that had survived their flight. It had been taken at the 1936 Olympics: a young girl in the uniform of the League of German Girls, beret at a jaunty angle over one ear. Jonathan had stuck it to the wall with a drawing pin. The last picture of his father, a young Wehrmacht lieutenant in field uniform and service cap, lay in a folder alongside Jonathan's birth certificate and bicycle insurance policy.

The tour would start in Danzig, said the letter from the Santubara Company. He would fly from Hamburg to Danzig, where the tour car would be waiting. He could then make notes at his leisure.

Danzig? thought Jonathan. He could use Danzig for his essay on Brick Gothic: 'The Giants of the North'. The Marien-kirche was one of the northern giants still missing from his collection. Lübeck, Wismar, Stralsund: he had seen these cities with their medieval colossi, and that was all well and good, but he had no first-hand sensory impression of Danzig, and it would be difficult for him to describe it in an essay.

If he accepted the commission he could kill two birds with one stone. As well as earning some money he would be acquiring knowledge at the same time, which, in turn, could later be converted into more money.

Jonathan washed his hands as meticulously as a surgeon, looking out of the window all the while. A class of school-children was swarming on the other side of the Isebek canal, a teacher anxiously herding them together – 'Don't fall in!' – while up in the sky a huge aeroplane was coming in to land at Fühlsbüttel.

I'm here in Hamburg, and I'm making a living, thought Jonathan. What's East Prussia to me? And a single great image arose in his mind's eye, of Uncle Edwin entering the church with the dead woman in his arms – where to put her? – and setting her down on the steps. The folds of her white dress stained with blood.

3

At three o'clock Ulla came to fetch her boyfriend so they could go for a walk. 'You need to air this room again,' she said. She stepped up behind him and turned over the papers on his desk to see what nonsense he had been writing. 'The nave is reminiscent of a womb' . . .? That really was the limit. She was wearing harem trousers and a men's waistcoat, unbuttoned, over her blouse.

Seeing her like that, Jonathan thought: All she needs is a turban. He himself had put on an unironed flannel shirt with a patterned suit and a black bow-tie. For a while he'd seriously considered donning the straw hat his friends said suited him so well.

There wasn't much going on down by the Elbe at this time of day. Young people were riding around on their bikes; teenagers who had grown up here and children whose mothers' corpses had not been set down in a church. A man was playing with his dog at the water's edge. He let the unsuspecting animal fetch the stick from the river, which was thick with cadmium. Some drunks were sitting on a bench with their bottles of vermouth, singing:

Oh, you lovely Westerwald
Where the wind whistles so cold
But the faintest ray of sun
Warms the heart like gold.

There was a woman with them. She was holding a tin of Chappi dog food and had extracted a chunk of meat with two fingers; she seemed to be about to put it in her mouth.

The wail of police sirens could be heard in the distance, along with chanting and shouting from a political demonstration that could have been mistaken for a football crowd. The big city! Everything here had its place – demonstrating, policing, looking on. Even the smashing of windows was tradition.

They walked along the Övelgönne, past what are known as the 'captains' houses'. Around the turn of the twentieth century retired seafarers had built them with their savings because they couldn't bear to be parted from the sea. Now the tiny cottages, each with its own little front garden, boathouse, arbour and flagpole, were worth millions and were under siege from property speculators. There were English cat figurines in the windows, ships in bottles and enormous shells picked up at the fish market. Some of the residents felt the need to explain themselves to passers-by: NUCLEAR POWER – NO THANKS was written on a piece of cardboard propped up against a garden gnome. The smell of food was all-pervasive: fillet of fish and sauerkraut soup.

There were no ships to be seen on the Elbe; they had set sail the previous night. These days no one could afford to stay in the harbour over the weekend.

Ships have something maternal about them, thought Jonathan; all that loading up and unloading . . . He imagined lying in a crate on a bed of hay and being lowered into the hold of a ship by crane. It was an appealing thought.

You couldn't really have said they were getting on well. The need to be civil on Ulla's special day resulted in them both coming out with spiky remarks such as 'But you said before' or 'Can't you talk about something else for a change? Don't you realize that gets on my nerves?' Ulla's habit of walking in step with Jonathan but half a metre ahead was also a source of friction. And there was dog shit all over the place; it was a wonder you didn't step in it, and sometimes you did.

Jonathan considered whether or not to tell his girlfriend about the invitation to East Prussia. It was on the tip of his tongue. Better not, he thought. Better to wait; she was sure to get jealous if she heard about it. Life with his girlfriend should have meant him running to his beloved, letter in hand, but it wasn't like that between them, which was a shame. Ulla Bakkre de Vaera always got nasty.

Ulla had something on her mind as well. A large bouquet of flowers had been delivered – a little too large, given that it had been ordered by her boss. She too should have run to her beloved and cried, 'Guess what – the old man's sent me flowers!' But she hadn't, and now it was too late.

They were just having another go at each other when they saw a sign on one of the little houses: ELBE GALLERY. So an artist had settled here. They must visit him!

They rang the bell, and the artist's wife opened the door. She had cuts and bruises on her face, inflicted by a husband outraged by his lack of success. On account of the privations of her marriage the poor woman had decided to be friendly.

Jonathan handed over two marks to her, and she practically curtsied. They stepped into the low-ceilinged house and surveyed the nature-themed paintings that hung in the living room. These depicted looming trees assailed by creepers. Here and there, for a bit of variety, the artist had painted branches sticking out to the right or left. Perhaps inspired by a need to imbue his nature studies with meaning, he had furnished the trees with human features. They were pretty hideous.

The painter had presumably heard plenty of negative comments about his work. At any rate, he sullenly shuffled out from the kitchen at the back, where a soup tureen stood on the table, it too sullen, almost mistrustful. He would have really liked to make a big entrance by smashing everything up with an axe, but he could always do that later.

The two visitors walked past the neatly painted, neatly framed pictures of gnarled trees, slowly at first then increasingly fast (two and a half thousand marks was a lot of money, after all), only half listening to the man's explanation of how with his tree paintings he had wanted to present a variation on Aesop's fable about not tormenting animals for fun. Trees were living things too, with souls and nerves that felt pain, if you carved a heart into their bark, for example. Living things – why wouldn't they have a soul? And we just chop them down. Trees can scream!

Ulla was more patient than her boyfriend. She didn't mind listening to the man, perhaps also because she could gaze at her reflection in the glass of the paintings. She parted her lips and studied her dead tooth.

Meanwhile, in a neighbouring room labelled MUSEUM, Jonathan discovered a collection of flotsam and jetsam. While the artist was telling Ulla that one million trees were felled in South America every day and asking her how much rent she reckoned he had to pay for the cottage in which he lived and whether she had any idea how expensive a single tube of cobalt blue was, Jonathan examined fragments of china in the flotsam museum, cup handles worn smooth by the sea, bits of leached wood, an old shoe. These remnants of human life roused him to lively, almost tearful enthusiasm, attracting his girlfriend's attention. What remnants of civilization would mankind discover and exhibit in a thousand years? asked Jonathan, regarding the little group with glistening eyes. He felt rather like a piece of flotsam himself, he said, and played the suffering card to his advantage: father killed on the Vistula Spit, mother breathed her last when he was born. Trek, icy wind, etc.

This interested the gallery owner, and he invited the young people to sit down. Where exactly had that been? he wanted to know, because he was from those parts himself. He too had trekked westwards, aged seven, in February '45. He still clearly remembered them finding a milk churn in a farmhouse, full of pork dripping. He'd never eaten such delicious pork dripping again in all his life.

Jonathan knew that the man was going to open up now, with all the charm of someone who usually acted tough. He had no desire to hear the dreadful stories the artist would have to tell. He'd had enough of shackles and chains. As Ulla sat down to take it in without distraction, he spotted a portfolio of watercolour paintings lying on a table. They'd been done by some children at a local school; a teacher had given his pupils the topic 'Environmental Protection' and had dropped their paintings off here. Whether or not they were art was questionable, but the money raised by selling them would go to Greenpeace. 'Good poison for all' it said on the portfolio. Jonathan studied the paintings, rejoicing at the originality with which the children had approached the subject. Good poison for all. What a thought!

It really was funny: cowboys drinking arsenic from bottles and exploding down below; cows, their front halves bloated into elephantine monsters, hindquarters dissolving in puddles of green slime. They were funny and frightful at the same time. And original. He called his girlfriend over: didn't she find it breathtaking too, this wealth of ingenuity?

'As long as young people keep showing this much imagination we don't need to worry about the future,' he said. And he pointed out to Ulla that these children's drawings were relevant to her subject: cruelty by way of thoughtlessness.

He waxed so enthusiastic about the lines and composition of the paintings that he ended up buying one for twenty-five marks. Greenpeace could use the money to buy itself some decent ballpoint pens.

After convincing themselves that there wasn't another bit of the house for them to look at – some sort of infernal machine in the cellar, perhaps – they said, 'So long!' to the artist and his wife. Over the course of the hour they had, in a way, become friends. The artist went on standing in the doorway for a long time, gazing across at the shipyard, which until just a few months ago had been full of sparks and clanging, but had now, unfortunately, been closed. An 8 per cent increase in wages had finished it off.

*

They sat in the Café Elbblick eating raspberry tart with whipped cream. The tart had been in the fridge and was ice-cold, the whipped cream was watery, the coffee weak and a pop singer was bawling from the loudspeakers.

The German proprietor, whom Jonathan summoned so he could complain, was not, in fact, the proprietor but an overworked employee who handed over the takings every evening to a foreign-looking man in a Mercedes. The cafe was gradually filling up, and he had no desire to discuss the topic of 'hospitality' with Jonathan. He recommended that if he didn't like it he should go elsewhere. 'Plenty of people come here who like our food.'

Ulla took the man's side. Did Jonathan actually have any idea how hard a waiter had to work? On his feet all day with people constantly moaning at him?

Jonathan countered that working at a steel furnace was presumably far more strenuous than working in a tourist restaurant with the sun shining up above and birds tweeting away. If he had to choose between bringing little girls fizzy drinks in a tourist restaurant and standing in seventy-degree heat every day for eight hours, he'd much rather walk around with a tray.

While Jonathan and Ulla were quarrelling the promenade was filling up with people of all ages who wanted to be seen as respectable citizens. They strolled from the Övelgönne to Blankenese, or the other way round, having taken to their cars to escape their trade-union groups. There were some demonstrators among them too, as the demonstration had ended at half past three; they were carrying reusable banners, folded and tucked under their arms, decent people who were very concerned about atmospheric pollution. They too wanted to enjoy nature here beside the Elbe, even if painters no longer needed cobalt blue to paint the river water. Incidentally, the abandoned shipyard over there – that was just typical! You could turn that into a cultural centre, with cabaret venues, self-help courses and hobby studios and rock concerts on summer evenings. Thousands of people were sure to come. What was the betting it'd all be knocked down? As if Germany hadn't seen enough rubble . . .

'Look at that guy!' said Jonathan, pointing to a man dressed for the demonstration, carrying a small child on his back who sported a communist beret. 'What sort of memories of early childhood will he dredge up for his psychiatrist in fifty years' time?'

Ulla also spotted some amusing sights. This was what they referred to as 'conducting research', and it brought them a little closer again. The Masuria question, the cheque and the bouquet flickered into their minds, but they held them at bay.

As entertainment for the weekend, the diffident waters of the Elbe were full of all kinds of amphibious cars, racing about and churning up soapy froth in front of and behind them. There was a huge variety of vehicles. The drivers waved to one another; surely Hamburg had never seen so many cars cruising about on the river. There were even some Dutch people here, with their pretty national flag, and Danes flying the *Dannebrog*. Television had sent people too; the camera crews were racing out in front in a couple of motorboats, spewing blue exhaust. Maybe they'd get lucky and there'd be an accident and, with luck, some casualties.

The occasion for this hectic sporting display, which pretty

much everyone was enjoying, was the big grey warship slowly ploughing up the Elbe. Military music could be heard in the distance, booming from a restaurant's loudspeakers to welcome this wonder of technology. This was a warship of peace: to demonstrate friendship between nations, it intended to drop anchor in the Hanseatic city that had been criminally destroyed by the Anglo-Americans and, of course, abysmally rebuilt by business-orientated German idiots. The cannon fore and aft were pointing at the sky, the big radar domes providing a formal contrast to the slim gun barrels. This contrast could not be said to be beautiful, because the spirit behind the technology was a diabolical one, but its aesthetic quality communicated itself to Ulla and Jonathan nonetheless.

'That ship is stuffed to the gunwales with electronics,' said Jonathan. And Ulla wondered whether women of easy virtue were waiting to satisfy the mariners' needs. She thought of the special sailors' trousers with a flap in the front.

Now the sailors, all dressed in white, were lining up on deck. Flags flew up the ropes, and commands were given in a strange way on special whistles. The drunks raised their bottles, and the sports enthusiasts lined up in their amphibious cars. After reaching the grey monster they turned elegantly and escorted the messenger of peace as they'd seen it done in photographs of the old days, when the *Queen Elizabeth* first arrived in New York harbour. The flotilla included an amphibious Volkswagen that had previously swum across the Dnieper and the Don. Every individual part had been replaced, but it was still the real thing.

Hark! Were they ringing the church bells? Was the church joining in this festival of peace – the progressive Hanseatic ministry that had, in the past, defied water cannon with crucifix and cassock? But no, this wasn't a special peal for peace; there was just a religious ceremony being performed in the church. A wedding, probably, thought Jonathan. He imagined aborted embryos borne before the bridal couple in little glass coffins, bedded on cotton wool and adorned with plastic flowers – for the glory of humankind, which was adopting a medically impeccable approach to ending the overpopulation of the planet.

He put the child's drawing – 'Good poison for all' – in a plastic wastepaper basket emblazoned with KEEP THE ENVIRONMENT CLEAN! in seven languages. He didn't want to be carrying the rolled-up paper around like a field marshal's baton.

It was, undoubtedly, a splendid sight, watching the gentle giant of a ship glide by. Everyone gathered on the promenade, as well as those sitting in cafes or at the panoramic windows of their villas up on the Elbchaussee, felt the same. Meanwhile, in the water, the fish struggled to breathe.

Just then a sort of pirate fleet came zooming across from the opposite bank, nippy little rubber dinghies fitted with outboard motors. They were crewed by people in orange, waving green buccaneers' flags, who had prepared themselves for every eventuality. As long as we live we will not tolerate warships here! Of any kind! A sea battle ensued between the rubber dinghy people and the amphibious cars, reminiscent of the fishermen's jousting on Lake Constance. The sports enthusiasts in the water cars were clearly coming off worse. Then the river police swept in, and the circling, honking mêlée slowly swam towards the harbour until there was nothing more for the spectators to see. Only the television people were still getting their money's worth. People would be able to watch the footage at home, and then they'd get to hear what they were supposed to make of the event.

4

That evening Jonathan and Ulla went to their local Turkish restaurant, the Ali Baba, which served kebabs made from the roasted flesh of rams that had been tortured to death. The texture was variable, from fatty to crisp; the meat was accompanied by sheep's cheese in oil with sliced onion rings on top, and, most importantly, it was not at all expensive. Maximum performance at minimal expense, plus extremely friendly service.

As regulars they were greeted effusively and led to a specially reserved corner divided off from the main restaurant by large, highly polished brass vessels. Their mutual friend Albert Schindeloe was already there waiting for them. An elderly bachelor in a beret and a rust-coloured polo neck, Schindeloe was an antiques dealer. He was the one who had sold Jonathan the Botero all those years ago. When Albert Schindeloe saw them, he leapt up and kissed Ulla's hand.

The candle on the table was lit with a lighter, and the Turkish waiter, a student from Ankara, made quite a fuss of Ulla. Albert Schindeloe had filled him in: this lady is celebrating her big day today, which means she's entitled to preferential treatment. The Turk even tried to kiss her, which was presumably the custom in his country; whatever the reason, Ulla didn't dare turn her head away as she did whenever Jonathan made an approach at the wrong moment.

Albert paid Jonathan no further attention; that was how things worked in this three-way friendship. The Turk, however, shook his hand and informed him that he had a checked jacket just like his; it was hanging in his wardrobe at home.

Ulla was looking delightful. Gentlemen at neighbouring tables turned their heads, thinking what a lucky devil Jonathan was to be going about with such a woman. Her round face in the candlelight, with its delicate features, her air of puzzled intellectuality, as if she were thinking: Where am I? What is this place? The little silver box engraved with flowers that Albert had just placed in front of her – was this for her? But why? He didn't have to do that! She was pleased with the present – 'Is it Biedermeier?' – as her mother had kept a similar little box for her milk teeth. She must have a look next time she visited, see if it was still there.

Jonathan accepted the admiration of the other customers unquestioningly. It was true: in these surroundings the pair of them did come across as rather impressive. He had once seen Chagall, in Paris; and here was Ulla with her splendid name . . . At the same time, however, Jonathan couldn't help thinking of the safety pin his girlfriend had used to fasten her blouse beneath her little jacket. She'd stuck Elastoplast in her shoes, too, to stop them flapping.

Soon their hunger was assuaged by tomato soup with melted cheese. The restaurant wasn't only inexpensive, it was also fast. The cheese trailed metre-long strands, prompting good-natured jokes about how, if necessary, you could always stand on a chair.

An agreeable mood prevailed, reinforced by the agreeable mood of the guests at the neighbouring table and the Ali Baba music issuing discreetly from four speakers, one in each corner. There was no need to be irritated by it, as it was impossible to judge its quality. Rather less pleasant were the pictures that hung on the walls between strings of glass prayer beads: chickens with bound feet, three men riding one small donkey and another who had seized his goat by the hind legs and was pushing it in front of him like a wheelbarrow. There were no photos on the wall of the Armenians who were driven out into the desert to die of thirst along with their wives and children.

Albert Schindeloe was their indispensable companion. His obscure past and mysterious financial circumstances made him interesting. Was he stinking rich or virtually bankrupt? Had he been in the SS or was he a communist? Was he from Thuringia or the Rhine? Probably all of the above. What was certain was that at some point he had tampered with a cheque, which had earned him a year and a half's so-called 'study vacation'. He loathed the current government as a result.

He loved Ulla, of course, but he also loved Jonathan. He had homosexual inclinations, and his way of expressing this to Jonathan was to be curt with him. He liked to call him 'Herr Schmidt', because surely Fabrizius – meaning 'craftsman' – was a Latinate version of Smith.

For their part, Ulla and Jonathan pronounced Schindeloe's first name in a Frenchified manner, which was their way of teasing him. '*Albair*' they would say – and with some justification, as it was Albert's custom to live in Paris from November until

March, selling to the French the stuff he couldn't shift in Germany.

It pained Albert that stupid people would call him 'Schinde*low*'. The insipid idiocy of that final syllable had accompanied him all his life, and it maddened him. 'Schindeloe', properly pronounced – *Schinder-lower* – sounded like the German for 'aloe' and made him think of frankincense and myrrh. Perhaps this was why he wore an Egyptian ring, a massive lump of copper-coloured gold he called 'the Ledger'. Ulla would very much have liked to know whether it was real, as real and old as her ring, which she would twist compulsively with her thumb whenever she was cornered. Once, years ago, she had asked if she might try the Ledger on and had been rebuffed. The magic would be lost, she was told; one might as well give it away.

The name Schindeloe never ceased to provide fresh topics of conversation whenever the three of them met up. A seminar would be held on the number of *Untermenschen* who had mispronounced it again, when really it was so terribly easy! *Schin – der – low – er*: how could you get it wrong? A very characterful name, incidentally, of Lower Saxon origin. 'Schindeloe' sounded like a witch-hunt, with its echoes of the German words for 'tumbrel' and 'bonfire'. How very fitting, then, that Albert was a redhead, the remnants concealed by his cat-hair-covered beret.

Ulla was also able to join in, her own name providing conversational fodder. 'Bakkre de Vaera' translated as 'behind the weir', so she was really Ulla Behindtheweir, or Hinterdemwehr. And if you shifted the gender '*Wehr*' could also mean 'weapons' – 'Ulla Hinter*der*wehr'. It made you think of chainmail and a sword; something Amazonian, anyway. Incidentally, Ulla was German through and through; you had to go back generations to find her Swedish origins.

'Cheers!' they said, and again, 'Cheers!' They knocked back the schnapps – which smelt of dishwasher and was laced with poisonous chemicals – and smacked their lips. The Turkish music created the right atmosphere. This restaurant was an oasis; who needed to go to Istanbul?

That was when it happened. A stone came flying in from the street, smashing a window and making a dent in a highly polished decorative samovar. People leapt to their feet and ran outside to grab the perpetrators; the cook even brandished a knife, yelling something about fascists and how their bellies should be slit open and boiling oil poured inside. Amid his unintelligible curses the word 'xenophobia' rang out loud and clear.

The birthday party pressed themselves to the window to watch the attacker being beaten up. Unfortunately there was nothing to be seen but traffic streaming indifferently past.

One by one the pursuers returned, the police were called, the roller blind was lowered in front of the broken windowpane and a girl from the kitchen swept up the shattered glass. People gradually calmed down, declaring from one table to another that it was a disgrace that fascism should be spreading again. Smashing the windows of the poor friendly Turks! What a pity they didn't catch those lads; they'd have been given such a hiding. They'd have been thrown to the ground and kicked to death. Or smacked till their cheeks were in shreds. Or pushed in front of an U-Bahn train.

Had they really been Nazis, though? That was the question. Perhaps they were unemployed people who were actually supporters of the Social Democratic Party but were being denied a more meaningful life. Or perhaps even fanaticized Turks from the other camp? Grey Wolves?

The little birthday party also considered various methods of killing, after which a degree of understanding was expressed, up to a point. Young hooligans did things like this – they had too much energy. Like students with their fencing duels around the beginning of the twentieth century. You had to adopt a loving approach to these youths, take them by the hand, speak to them kindly. They needed people in authority with psychological training, job-creation schemes, a programme of leisure activities and so on. We weren't averse to a bit of fun ourselves in our youth. Smashing windows was tradition, a silly boys' prank. When you looked at America, that was a whole different ballgame – they'd wipe out the entire restaurant. Dear God! Albert Schindeloe confessed to having tortured a great many frogs – it's just the way boys are . . . And Ulla Bakkre de Vaera was able to tell them about decapitating cockchafers; you just flicked off the head with your finger. She laughed as she said it but stopped abruptly because it exposed her dead tooth.

Jonathan had never done anything of the sort. He had only ever beaten up his teddy bear.

Albert owned a corner shop on Lehmweg where he sold his antiques. Clocks of all sizes, old spectacles, all kinds of carafes, tin figurines and medals. Browsers could pick things up in his shop for five marks, and from this Albert Schindeloe made a living. In addition, he received some mysterious income, pensions or compensation payments which were nobody else's business.

They went over to his place briefly after the meal, to please him. Above the shop, its windows crammed with wares and protected by strong bars, he owned a little studio that was also bursting at the seams with junk he was either unwilling or unable to let go. Chairs were cleared; two cats came up, purring, and the visitors glanced around in discreet astonishment. Beside a folded-out family altar, its cross missing the Crucified, and a box of votive figures' silver arms and legs was a cardboard box with a rubber tap. From this Albert drew red wine into glasses, which he cleaned for his guests with a handkerchief, and they sat around telling stories. Albert told them what he had coaxed out of whom and how there were customers who would declare, 'I've already got that painting.' There was the clock scheme in the 1960s – the shipping of hundreds of pendulum clocks to America. And the silver boom in the 1970s when those crazy Americans bought up silver by the hundredweight and came a terrible cropper.

He'd love to go through French people's apartments, Albert said; see whether he could find any loot confiscated in Stuttgart by French infantrymen during the First World War. He had an image in his mind of a delightful little girl's head, in marble, sitting on a mantelpiece. Where could it be? Lyons, perhaps? 'You wouldn't believe all the stuff that turned up again in Moscow.'

Perhaps he could travel to Moscow and look around the flea markets. The Russians were sure to be happy to get their hands on foreign currency. 'Watches! Watches!' You must still be able to pick up wartime wristwatches over there, he was sure of it.

It was getting late by the time Albert opened various drawers containing all sorts of medals and spectacles from the 1920s and 30s. Heaven knows who had worn them. Hundreds of pairs of spectacles.

He probably has drawers full of cut-off hair here too, thought Jonathan.

When they got home they said, 'Goodnight, then,' and went to their respective rooms. The toilet flush rang out, and Jonathan wound his watch. He thought of the little Turkish woman at the Ali Baba whom he had glimpsed briefly as she swept up the shattered glass, the chef's trousers with the little checks, the white cap on her head. He looked in the mirror over the basin and wondered whether he made any impression on a woman like her, with or without his straw hat.

He flung himself on to his leather sofa and reached for a book on the basilica in Trier. It was a brick construction but had nothing else in common with the northern goddesses, their wide pelvises squatting over the little houses of medieval towns. Good to the left, wicked to the right, thought Jonathan; that was how it should be in churches, and those who streamed in departed feeling enriched.

Just then he heard a two-fingered whistle from the adjoining room. This was his girlfriend's way of letting him know that she still expected something of the day.

At moments like these Jonathan hated her childishness, her efficacious grin and bony frame. He hated the fact that he was called upon to devote himself to her three times a week. But, as he walked along the sweetish-smelling, mildewed corridor to her room, desire rose up in him after all, as it always did when she summoned him: a kind of 'oh well, why not?' response. He groped his way into her room with its orange-red glow and allowed himself to be pulled into her bed, to be welcomed by naked arms, complacent laughter. Breathing hard, he set about the act that was supposed to be pleasurable for him, and ultimately was; she issued precise instructions, and he followed them with increasing satisfaction.

When it was over he was abruptly dismissed. Ulla Bakkre de Vaera turned her broad back on him and rolled on to her side, his cue to depart. He collected himself and fumbled his way back to his room, where he threw himself on to his lovely sofa and heaved a deep sigh. *Et in Sion habitatio eius!*

Now the general's widow could also set aside her volume of poetry and take her sleeping pill. There was nothing more to be expected of the day.

5

Early the following week Jonathan found an opportunity to say, 'Incidentally . . .' Ulla was in the middle of throwing away a large bouquet of flowers when he told her of the Santubara Company's unusual offer and that he couldn't really see any reason not to go.

Ulla Bakkre de Vaera received the information with indifference. Her response was along the lines of 'All right for some,' but barely even that. Eventually she said, 'Well, you know best,' and although Jonathan didn't know what to make of this remark, it set him thinking. Is driving around East Prussia risky? he wondered, as he helped her stuff the flowers into the rubbish bin.

My friend, thou'lt win
More in this hour to soothe thy senses
Than in the year's monotony . . .

'You know best.' What did she mean by that?

Although Jonathan had not yet given the Santubara Company a definite yes, he was starting to take more of an interest in the east. He learnt that the landscape there was gently undulating, dotted with dozens of lakes that had formed from dead ice. Winter rye, potatoes, buckwheat. He read a wide range of historical papers and spent a whole afternoon learning about Tannenberg, one battle lost there in the fifteenth century by the Teutonic Knights and another won by Hindenburg in his glorious victory of 1914 ('He evened the score . . .').

He read up on how southern East Prussia had voted in the plebiscites. Pro-Germany in 1920! This pleased him. He read statements by the Ministry for Displaced Persons declaring that, from a legal point of view, the country still belonged to Germany. He browsed art history books, reading about Marienburg on the Nogat, not a northern giant by his definition but still a brick building of ludicrous size, to be considered alongside the Marienkirche in Danzig.

Since Jonathan had begun to focus on it he had started to get the impression that the whole of Hamburg was peopled with refugees and displaced persons: Sudeten Germans, Silesians, Pomeranians, West Prussians and East Prussians – East Prussians especially. The woman at the butcher's who sliced the fat off the meat with a sharp knife, Dr Doysen from the university library, his colleague Rothermund in the editorial office – he actually came from Memel, which the Lithuanians got their hands on completely illegitimately, but no one remembered that any more. Hamburg was teeming with East Prussians, every one of whom must have a story to tell, and it seemed to Jonathan very strange that nobody asked them about it. None of the glossy magazines that clamoured for tales of blood and murder were interested in these stories. Love and peace and harmony were what they looked for with regard to their neighbours in the east.

There was Frau Krumbach, for example, who mopped the stairs every day. It turned out that she was from just outside Rastenburg in East Prussia; she'd left when she was fourteen. Jonathan spoke to her as she scoured the terrazzo floor, and while he gazed absent-mindedly at the empty niches in the stairwell walls (the architect had put them in eighty years earlier to hold paintings, allegorical depictions of the four points of the compass – 'East, west, home's best' – which for some reason had never been delivered) she told him about a lake. She had grown up on its shores; what a beautiful lake it had been. She would walk out of the house in the morning and the lake would be right there, spread out in front of her, silver and winking. Rowing boats, swimming, fishing . . . they'd always referred to it as 'our lake'.

'When will we be able to go back?'

Her father had been a fisherman, and in winter he would leave a wooden stake to freeze in the water; then he'd hammer a nail in the top and fasten a rope to it to make a merry-go-round for the children. The ice had been so clear you could see the fish motionless beneath.

Will we ever get East Prussia back? she wanted to know; but Jonathan didn't know either.

The newsagent from whom Jonathan bought his *Rundschau* every morning – JAPANESE INSIST ON RETURN OF KURIL ISLANDS – was unfriendly at first when Jonathan asked whether he too might be from East Prussia: he thought he could detect it in his accent. Might he be able to tell him what it was like there? The newsagent declined. No, no, he wanted nothing to do with it. Forget it. Those Polacks were incapable of doing anything, and now, to cap it all, we were supposed to help them! After a while, though, he abandoned his cover girls, cheap war novellas and television magazines with the latest gossip about newsreaders and their favourite food, stepped out of his kiosk and told his tale. His father had owned a stationer's in Heilsberg: pencil sharpeners and notepaper. The Poles had sent him to a camp – never heard from him again – and his mother had died of sepsis. He'd found himself all alone in the world at twelve years of age. He'd roamed around, surviving by begging.

Then the man came out with stories so horrific it really made you wonder why they didn't get written up in the magazines he sold: labour camp, prison, beatings. And as he recounted his experiences (not without a feel for the drama), a picture formed in Jonathan's mind: his Uncle Edwin entering the church with his dead mother in his arms and the sun breaking through a stained-glass window, slanting in from above.

The newsagent's horror stories culminated (by which time several people had gathered to listen) in the description of his escape from Poland in 1948. He had swum across the River Oder. The East German police had immediately sent him back – or rather, turned him in. His own people! Him! To the Poles!

The man grew increasingly agitated. A little dog that cocked its leg on his kiosk was given a kick. Finally he started mocking a television programme about Masuria: the wonderful collective farms the Poles had over there and the terrific factories, and they were such great people, the Poles . . . Those television people should come and talk to him; he'd have a thing or two to tell them. Care packages! Reparations!

By the time he had finished the man had red blotches on his neck, and other memories started welling up from beneath the ancient wound. On Sunday mornings he'd had to weed between the cobbles in front of the church, and the Poles who went to Mass there, Catholics like him, had spat at him. As these words burst out of him he pounded his chest, a martyr through and through.

Jonathan realized he had forfeited his advantage on the suffering front. He stood at the kiosk in his baggy Danish cardigan, tugging at his nostrils, wondering how to get away.

He usually visited antiquarian bookshops in search of material about Flemish town houses and city gates in Mecklenburg. Now he went looking for an old Baedeker guide to East Prussia. He sorted through albums of cigarette cards, newspapers, *Art in the Third Reich*. The extremely nice bookseller told him that there was a very inexpensive reprint of the East Prussian Baedeker and sold him, for a few marks, the handwritten biography of a woman from Königsberg entitled *Sunny Days*. 'Otherwise we just throw this kind of stuff away,' said the bookseller, who was not East Prussian but originally from Bavaria.

Afterwards Jonathan visited the world-renowned Dr Götze bookshop, which specialized in maps of all kinds. Here you could find not only globes of the moon and Mars that lit up inside but also city maps of Buenos Aires and Moscow. This was where Arctic explorers came to equip themselves, where sailing enthusiasts purchased nautical charts of the Kattegat.

A Herr Hofer laid out in front of Jonathan maps of East Prussia – 'currently under Polish administration' – with coats of arms left and right, some showing the 1945 evacuation routes. These maps were wonders of precision, with a scale of 1:300,000, showing the Vistula Lagoon and the Curonian Lagoon. All the place names were still in German.

'Be careful, though,' said Herr Hofer. 'You're not allowed to take German maps into Poland. You could get into trouble.'

Jonathan asked for everything of interest to be packed up (although he turned down recordings of songs from the homeland). He also bought *Documentation of the Expulsion*, a five-volume paperback collection of first-class atrocities, on special offer. He could give it to Ulla later, for Christmas. He couldn't carry it around openly, reading it on the U-Bahn, for instance; people would take him for a Cold War fanatic.

He cashed his uncle's cheque and went to the Oyster Cellar, where all kinds of eccentrics liked to lunch. He ordered a plate of mussels in aspic with sautéed potatoes and leafed through *Sunny Days,* in which the now eighty-year-old author told of how, as a child, she used to run through meadows whooping with joy. Jonathan wondered why he hadn't taken an interest in his homeland long ago. He supposed it was because East Prussia wasn't his homeland: his home was Bad Zwischenahn – the furniture factory, where his uncle's workers used to let him ride on their shoulders, and the lake, where he had paddled in the afternoons and skated in winter.

A wooden stake frozen into the ice: that would have been fun.

His uncle's study, where he had lain on the sofa when he had mumps. The top left-hand drawer of the desk, in which he had loved to rummage as a child. The pit of wood shavings he and his friends had tumbled into as children. And a winter morning on the lake, a ball of sun through the fog, more beautiful than anything any artist might paint today.

The longer he thought about it the clearer his 'homeland' became to him. But did he yearn for it? No, because he still had it.

*

In the days that followed Jonathan spent hours lying on the sofa, studying the map of East Prussia in a singularly uncomfortable position. He lay on his back and held the map above his head, but it kept flopping down. In the end he spread it out on the table and marked in red felt-tip pen the cultural stops he planned to suggest to the Santubara Company people: Marienburg, Frauenburg, Braunsberg, Heilsberg. It really was unbelievable that the Russians had cut themselves a piece of the Vistula Spit as well. What did the Poles have to say about that?

Pillau: the refugees' last resort as they fled the victors' revenge. Jonathan pictured a line of evacuees trudging across the frozen lagoon, the heads of horses that had fallen through the ice still sticking out of the water, low-flying planes of the glorious Red Army roaring past overhead, tracer bullets slamming into the miserable procession. And then there were the overcrowded ships. The carts left behind on the quay, the horses still in harness, hanging their sad heads. You could even see a goat in one of the photos.

Jonathan picked up the written account again, *Sunny Days*. Homeland? No, impossible, you couldn't say that any more. It smacked of nationalist propaganda.

He didn't go to visit his uncle, who would only have reeled off endless anecdotes. He didn't go to Bad Zwischenahn because he was afraid he would be given nostalgic errands to run on his trip. He didn't even *need* to go, because the more he thought about not going the more of the old stories he remembered. His uncle didn't need to tell him anything about East Prussia; he knew it all, including the things he hadn't told him yet.

He just gave him a quick call, asked about Rosenau and

made a note of where it was so he wouldn't forget, scatterbrained as he was. He learnt that his uncle's old estate was situated in the Russian zone. Thank God, he thought, in that case I don't have to go there as well.

One afternoon at half past four he took a sheet of paper and wrote to the Santubara Company. Yes, he would do it; he would go. By now he was quite looking forward to this exotic enterprise. He could visit Italy or Spain later; they weren't going anywhere.

Five thousand marks plus expenses, which were negotiable. Would they reimburse him for maps and books? It would be good to know.

6

Ulla was seldom home these days; the exhibition was very demanding, she said. From time to time she would stand in the doorway and shake her head at Jonathan. She had nothing against his studies, but when she saw him lying like that on the sofa, a paper cup of lemonade on the table, he looked so *discarded* – wrecked, even. He kept getting smaller and smaller in her eyes, the dingy room bigger and bigger.

Jonathan registered that she was standing in the doorway, telling him that she really had to go now and wouldn't be back until late. And as she closed the door behind her, he thought: What did she say?

He stared into space, and had the sense that it was not him doing the thinking – the thinking was happening inside him. Order was being created in his brain as if in a carousel vending machine.

When he'd had his fill of pictures and numbers he was suddenly overcome by a feeling that enough was enough. He hauled himself up and went to see Albert Schindeloe on Lehmweg.

'Is it Tuesday or Wednesday today?' he asked his friend, who had been planning to spend a peaceful afternoon entering a few select receipts in an accounts ledger and throwing the others in the wastepaper basket. With the two of them alone together Albert showed his nicer side. He was friendly, and when he stroked his fat tomcat it was as if he were stroking Jonathan.

Out of all the stuff hanging, standing and lying around in Albert's shop – the piano candleholders, the glasses and ceramics, the medals and helmets – there wasn't a single item Jonathan would have wanted. The little 1930s porcelain figurine on Albert's desk perhaps: a modern girl standing, rather stiffly, on a gilded ball. He took the thing in his hand, held it up to the light and turned it as people do in films. The figurine weighed surprisingly little; it was hollow.

Albert set aside his confidential ledger receipts and asked Jonathan whether he would dare to take a crowbar and break off the tiles in the stairwell of the Isestrasse building? If the house had been destroyed in the war the tiles would all have been lost anyway. Twenty marks a tile; how about it?

This suggestion was doomed to failure, not least because Jonathan was a person devoid of practical skills. Also, he didn't want to lose the raised water lilies he ran his finger along when charging up and down the stairs.

The general's widow probably wouldn't care either way if someone stole the tiles, Albert said. But Jonathan refused: some reflex prevented him from carrying out this knavery. And imagine the racket! In the stairwell, breaking off tiles with a crowbar! In principle, yes, sure, but no. He'd prefer to fill the empty niches in the stairwell with allegories of the four corners of the earth and add something to the house rather than take something away.

Albert Schindeloe resisted starting another conversation

about the Botero; he didn't want to spoil his own and Jonathan's good mood.

Their conversation was interrupted by a man who wanted to change a hundred-mark note. He spoke to Albert as if he knew him well. When he heard about Jonathan's Polish enterprise he advised him to take five-mark coins with him; they counted as small change, he said, so you didn't have to declare them on entry.

A housewife from Rahlstedt with nothing better to do came in looking for two cups for her set of porcelain – 'You know, the one with those roses all over it.' She already had saucers.

Did she mean kitchen porcelain or living-room porcelain? Albert asked her. Or was she, perhaps, in search of a chamber pot?

When she had gone – the two men were pleased that they didn't have any porcelain with 'those roses' all over it – a pensioner entered the shop. In his trembling hand he carried a plastic bag with a Bible and hymnal. Might these be something for Albert? he asked. They were ancient family treasures, very valuable.

Albert leafed through the Bible – a 1904 edition – and read aloud:

I have surely seen the affliction of my people which are in Egypt, and have heard their cry by reason of their taskmasters . . .

The old man was dealt with kindly, but they turned him away and watched him go with a sort of sadness. Albert blamed the bloody government for this man having to sell his Bible and hymnal; they spent billions on missiles but were constantly cutting pensions! Albert's worldview derived partly from tabloid newspapers and partly from some obscure Trotskyite pamphlet that he hid under his files whenever anyone entered the shop.

At midday they went out for potato soup. The best one was to be found at the Spanish place, which wasn't actually Spanish at all. This restaurant was run, pretty dreadfully, by a couple of very German students, and their only satisfying dish was a local German potato soup. The young man poured their beers in a manner that seemed to be saying: Look! I can do this too. He was a bit too cocky. And the famous poster of the German soldier shooting a woman with a child in her arms hung on the wall of the loo.

NO MORE WAR!

It couldn't be a German, people used to say; his cap was all wrong. And as proof of the photographer's unscrupulousness they would cite Capa's famous photo from the Spanish Civil War of a soldier falling, hit by the fatal bullet. That had been a set-up, they would say, a spur-of-the-moment thing, taken well behind the front line, with the comrades eating breakfast and splitting their sides laughing.

Back in the days when the Spanish place still had a Spanish owner, all the local dealers used to meet here: Heinzi, the man with the bicycle; Dr Ommel, the clock collector, who was also an expert on chinoiserie and fluent in Japanese; Giorgiu, the glass specialist, who gave everything away on credit and nicked things from his colleagues. The police had been round to see him again recently; people were talking about it.

None of these colourful characters ate at the Spanish place any more because the restaurant had gone downhill. Potato soup isn't to everyone's taste.

Jonathan and Albert were still discussing the woman from Rahlstedt and her rose-covered porcelain. She was probably a divorced dentist's wife whose husband would have to support her for the next fifty years even though things had never been any good between them in bed. The two friends were of the opinion that stupid women really were quite remarkably stupid, a theoretical view unsubstantiated by any practical experience and expressed only when they were alone together.

Towards the end of the little meal Albert took a roll of fifty-mark notes from his jacket pocket and asked his friend if he could bring him back a few of those Polish wooden Jew figurines or some old amber jewellery.

The next morning Jonathan decided to pay a visit to the general's widow. East Prussian, eighty years old – perhaps she could provide him with some background information that would be useful for his article. He pictured the sleigh rides this woman might have gone on as a child to her uncle on his neighbouring estate: rosy cheeks, wolves perhaps running behind the sleigh, and then the horses stumble, and the beasts sink their fangs into the bellies of the noble animals and warm blood gushes forth.

He knocked on the door, and after a while it was opened. The general's widow was a gaunt woman with pale-blue eyes and a crown of white curls framing a girlish face cross-hatched with wrinkles. She was not in the least surprised to find the young man, who could have come to see her long ago, paying her a visit on a Wednesday morning at quarter past eleven. She let him into her dark suite of rooms, offered him a cracked 1950s armchair, sat down on the couch, which was covered in books and newspapers, and put her feet up. A crudely tinted, large-format photograph of her husband in his general's uniform hung above the sofa, and in front of her, on the little crescent-shaped table, stood a portable typewriter that looked as if it had probably come from the Wehrmacht supply room. She had clearly been writing something; there was a piece of paper on the roller, and the cigarette she had set aside sent a vertical column of smoke up into the air. Beyond the sepulchral living room the other rooms, glimpsed through open sliding doors, conveyed a sense that someone had just been in there searching for weapons.

Jonathan was extremely courteous. He informed her that he too was from East Prussia, sort of – Rosenau, perhaps she'd heard of the place? During the evacuation he had, as it were, 'lost' his mother, which was to say that she had breathed her last, or rather bled to death, after his birth. He asked after the health of the esteemed general's widow, who had borne seven children with scarcely a problem: merchants, bankers, a clerk in an industrial firm, and Jonas, the golden boy, who was married, lived in California and asked her for money from time to time. He would have liked to address the general's widow, as she sat there looking at him, as 'Excellency', or at the very least 'Madame', but couldn't bring himself to do it. Those blue eyes, that crown of white curls . . . although smoking like a chimney didn't really go with the teenager look.

To give the old lady time to focus on the past Jonathan said how wonderful it was to be living here in the house on Isestrasse and how strange that the two of them had never exchanged a word before now. Such a thing would never happen in southern countries, he said, crossing his legs. In southern countries people were much friendlier. Recently, on Lake Garda – how he'd enjoyed that! – the people had invited him to join a funeral celebration: such natural good cheer! They'd offered him wine and cake, even though the Wehrmacht had shot thirteen men from the village in a nearby railway tunnel. Hamburg was more aloof: it seemed it was unheard of here to show consideration for other human beings. The other day he'd asked a man at a phone box if he had any change and had been completely ignored.

As he was talking he let his eyes wander round the room. Good grief, what a mess. Beside the sofa stood a glass cabinet full of china, its cracked pane taped up with sticking plaster. There were some little paintings on the wall that were really not bad, technically sound – an avenue, a lake with trees and swans – and then there were van Gogh's inevitable sunflowers mounted on compressed cardboard.

Who's going to inherit all these pictures? thought Jonathan. He wondered why the lady didn't just take one down and give it to him. You don't need pictures any more when you're that old!

The general's widow probably thought he'd come about the rent; that he wasn't able to pay it. She lit a new cigarette from the butt of the old one and heard instead that Jonathan had to – and, of course, wanted to – go to Poland, East Prussia to be precise, and was gathering general information about the region.

Books didn't tell him the things he needed to know about local customs, superstitions. No doubt she had invaluable knowledge to impart. His generation was completely uninformed about these matters.

The general's widow took a sip of coffee, which was surely cold by now, from her stained cup. The saucer remained stuck to the bottom. 'Dear God, yes, East Prussia,' she said. But before telling him that she was currently in the midst of writing it all down for her grandchildren she complained that the foliage outside her window, the trees on the street, stopped the sunlight getting in. She felt like a night owl! Her only consolation was that every other house had chestnuts outside; only hers, number 13, had a plane tree. So hers was the exception! This plane tree reminded her of the park on her uncle's estate – Heiditten, 1938 – where she'd spent so many wonderful days.

'All chestnuts,' she said in her deep voice. 'One after another. My house is the only one with a plane tree outside.' It was nice, but a bit crazy too, she said, and typical of Hamburg City Council. Her life had been full of special things, crazy things. In East Prussia, back in '45, the people on the neighbouring estates had been killed by Red Army soldiers. Only she was spared. The soldiers had been about to start their looting; they were already pointing the gun at her when an officer of the guard came along with his staff, threw those fellows out, moved in with her and protected her. It was a blessing, of course, that she could speak Russian.

Along he came and lived in her house. There was roasting and frying and piano playing in the evenings. And then he'd more or less conducted her out. 'You can't stay here,' he'd said, and had driven her in a car across Polish territory to Stettin. She could still see him standing there at the border. Incredible: she still thought about it today.

Her husband had had an inkling early on of what was in store for East Prussia. His realism had not been clouded. Imagine: he'd bought this house in the summer of 1944, transferred crates and crates of books and paintings here and all the silver. Her cousin in Bonn had rescued nothing but the clothes she stood up in. Not a single item. Whereas she had rescued pretty much everything.

Crazy.

On the windowsill, where an ancient bouquet of flowers was scattering its petals over dead flies, stood frames full of photographs: the highly decorated husband, the children and she herself, a young woman with a crown of blonde curls. Yes – this young girl was, without a doubt, the general's widow, sixty years ago.

Jonathan stared at it in amazement. A powerful yearning rose up in him for a time when white manor houses gazed out over golden fields of corn, and a young officer came riding up and was expected at the gate.

On the writing desk lay an old photo album, bound in faded green velvet with brass corners and clasps. The general's widow asked him to pass it to her. She leafed through, explaining the pictures to Jonathan, who came to stand beside her: the whitewashed house, covered in vine tendrils, with the donkey cart in front; her sisters in little sailor dresses; her father out hunting with Hindenburg.

Then she told him stories. Her upbringing had been strict: unheated bedrooms in winter, but on birthdays her mother would tie a ribbon around her arm with a big blue bow. If you were wearing a blue ribbon, everyone knew that today was your birthday.

The general's widow went on like this, lighting cigarette after cigarette, each from the butt of the last, and Jonathan thought: What a shame no one's interested in these stories nowadays. He wasn't interested in them either, but he did think it was a strange situation, him sitting here one Wednesday in August, in the room of a survivor, an ancient relic. The younger generation listening at the feet of Age – though not indefinitely, of course. He must drop it into his next conversation with Albert Schindeloe that he was always chatting to old people; it was important to look out for them, after all.

One story followed another. Time passed. Finally the grand-children were counted off – one married in Canada, one a lawyer for Bayer in Leverkusen – and Jonathan wished he were far, far away. In his room, on his nice leather sofa. What on earth had he been thinking of, letting himself in for this?

'Do go to East Prussia, Herr Fabrizius,' said the general's widow, rising to her feet. 'It'll be a journey you'll never forget.'

With the visit concluded Jonathan went back to his room and threw himself on to his sofa. It was curious, he thought; she'd been drawing a pension for forty years now, not to mention compensation for her losses during the war. How many generals' wives were there, all of them drawing pensions? It was extra-ordinary that the national economy could afford it. Then he considered that other people received pensions and benefits too, and that ultimately the recipients of these pensions and benefits went out and spent the money. They used it to buy cigarettes, for example, or coffee, or immersion heaters; and those merchants used it to pay the wages and salaries of their employees, who in turn bought cigarettes and coffee and got themselves a new stereo.

So who loses out in the end? thought Jonathan, getting tangled up in his own reasoning.

7

Jonathan would have liked to spend his last evening sitting quietly with Ulla listening to the Piano Concerto in E-flat major and browsing through one of her neatly compiled cruelty folders (the positioning of the feet of the Crucified!), but for some reason it wasn't possible. Ulla was restless. She was prowling up and down beside the wall unit and glancing out of the window, almost as if she were expecting someone. She said she had to work anyway; she had to go through everything with Dr Kranstöver again at the museum at eight o'clock to make final preparations for the exhibition. There were more testimonies of acts of cruelty than you would think. Cannibals in Africa and Central America; people being flayed alive; she must send a telex to Mexico. Cruelty? The subject was infinite.

Jonathan decided to go to a piano recital. The pianist Stepanskaya was playing Chopin and Debussy at the Kleines Haus, which was just right for this evening.

Ulla had the record *Children's Corner*; it had long been part of her evening repertoire. She also had a record of Chopin's Études, and it was hard to believe ten fingers were enough to create such a din.

Jonathan would be spared that this evening: various Chopin Nocturnes were on the programme but no Études. It also included the beautiful ballads in G-minor that made you think, oh, I could play this too, and then suddenly got incredibly complicated. This music should be played to young people who otherwise preferred to ruin their hearing in discos, to prove to them that classical music does have its charms.

The organizer had arranged for real candles to be placed on the theatre's (rather battered) grand piano, and Stepanskaya was wearing a yellow silk dress which she had spread out far behind her. As she sat on her stool, collecting herself for a moment, her dark hair fell forward, making her appear desirable although she was quite advanced in age. Then she raised her head, wrung her hands as if in prayer and suddenly pounced on the keys.

That intimate space, the atmospheric lighting, the mostly refined audience leaning in slightly to get closer to the music or leaning back as if the enharmonic changes were fanning them with a balmy evening breeze: Jonathan took it all in. There were students with prominent Adam's apples accompanied by their girlfriends, and little girls who would, it might be hoped, find piano lessons more palatable after this; there were very old people with hearing aids, thinking of their parental homes – Mother, ah yes, how beautiful she was; and Father would stand beside her at the piano – 'Chant sans paroles' – turning the pages. Towards all of these people the molten music flowed along prepared, receptive channels.

This is Western culture, thought Jonathan. He hoped the people sitting to the left and right of him could tell that he too belonged to Western culture and was contributing to it with his work, beyond the waving wheatfields of music, from one intellect to another. That he was not above travelling to East Prussia purely out of interest and possibly being mugged by someone who took a shine to his watch.

He listened to the music, testing his memory to see whether he recognized the chords and runs. Why don't I own a house beside a lake? he wondered: white, behind a copper beech tree, with steps leading down to the water, the bottom one sculpied by little lapping waves. He would sit on a white bench in front of the cool white house, and the open windows would spill forth the music he was listening to now, music you could no longer really listen to with a clear conscience. In the deserts of Africa refugees drag themselves through the sand, plagued by hunger and thirst, only to end up living on rubbish tips in the cities.

Sitting so close to others in the confines of the small room made it hard for Jonathan to concentrate and allow himself to be transported. These people hadn't all come for the music; they were already familiar with it. They had come to wallow in their own memories and to experience something that might become part of history, so that one day they'd be able to say: I was there, I experienced it – the concert when Stepanskaya played those beautiful, melancholy moonlit runs, up and down, sent them out into the concert hall, then collapsed over the keys. She was rumoured to be incurably ill.

It made Jonathan uncomfortable, this physical proximity to people who smelt of old cigar smoke or exuded clouds of powder and perfume and were fervently hoping Stepanskaya would meet her maker that night. In front of him a child even demanded, quite audibly, to sit on its mother's lap – 'Mummy, is it nearly over?' Yet he also found the proximity to these people appealing, people whose minds were now creating images to go with the music, like an interior film playing to the score of F-sharp minor and A major. These were people of intellect, not the kind who holidayed on the Cornish cliffs and said afterwards, 'It was nice.' People who cared about culture and made sure it didn't die, who were prepared to pay fifteen marks to hear compositions to which they could, in part, have hummed along.

Unlike the concert-goers to his right and left, Jonathan did not see moonlit nocturnal forests. He regretted that the score wasn't on a moving band above the curtain so he could follow whether it was about to go up or down. Instead, he accompanied the music with thoughts about Chopin's blood-spitting latter years. A monk's cell shaped like a coffin, in a damp monastery on Majorca. Exploited by the locals, rain all day and all night, then travelling on to London – such foolhardiness.

He also thought about George Sand, that incorrigible trouser-wearing woman who initially tended to Chopin before leaving him in the lurch. Did she also give a two-fingered whistle on certain occasions?

As the mortally ill Stepanskaya hammered out the melancholy chords, Jonathan was walking through the damp Carthusian monastery with the blood-spitting composer, filled with foreboding. Perhaps he would be murdered in Poland? His skull split by an axe; or a knife to the stomach? He saw himself lying spreadeagled on the ground in a forest, throat cut, a Central European sacrificial lamb.

*

Then it was Debussy's turn, with his underwater music. Despite the fact that he had been a savage hater of Germans, the audience loved him. 'Clair de lune' . . . This was the memory of summer evenings with no mosquitoes, evenings when you didn't need to go back indoors to fetch a blanket or think about the office tomorrow; evenings spent, instead, recalling long-forgotten memories. If one ignored the ridiculous occasions for which Debussy created pieces of music – 'Golliwog's Cakewalk' – these impressionistic sounds were indispensable to the soul. It was a pity you couldn't hang them on the wall like van Gogh's sunflowers.

One of the pieces Ms Stepanskaya played was called 'The Sunken Cathedral'. According to the programme you could clearly hear the cathedral ascending from the depths, little by little, finally rising up in glory before the eyes of mankind.

The woman stopped playing, and the rhythmic applause began, interspersed with occasional cries of 'Bravo!' in acknowledgement of her playing so energetically despite her treacherous heart defect. Twenty years of practising scales, memorizing all the Nocturnes, Schumann, Debussy, Mussorgsky, and soon to be pushing up the daisies. Those well-trained hands forcibly folded by the corpse washer. First the flesh falls away, then the maltreated sinews . . . There might have been some who were sorry the virtuoso had not been carried off stage to her deathbed like Lipatti, or – better still – collapsed as she played, up there in the candlelight, her life ending with a clashing chord. 'I was there, I saw it happen . . .'

As this had not come to pass, they applauded. The pictures in their heads vanished, and Western culture evaporated. Now they had to hit the road, so off they went into the open air to catch the next U-Bahn or steer the car through the traffic out to the blessed suburbs, where they switched on the television and watched the late-night news.

Jonathan was placated by the fact that others were also jostling to get out into the fresh air, faster than seemed fitting for such a velvety evening. And then he realized: isolation – me here, you there – is what characterizes Western culture. Yet it's in doing things together that we overcome our loneliness.

Temporarily, at least.

As Jonathan mounted his bicycle he resolved that he would keep on with his work. He wouldn't just bring his northern giants to light, little by little, he would do all sorts of detailed work as well. Provençal fences, bridge parapets of 1920s Chicago, why Wittgenstein boxed the ears of the pupils in his village school, the significance of the semi-quavers in Robert Schumann's diaries . . . and East Prussia. He would write an article about the region that would blow people away. It wouldn't be suited to witty authorial readings in the local accent, it wouldn't languish in the archives of the homeland associations, a testimony of attachment to the native soil; instead it would be picked out of the monotonous expanses of text in the daily newspapers. Have you read this? people would say. Fabrizius has written about Masuria.

At around the same time Ulla Bakkre de Vaera was sitting on a restaurant terrace by the Alster with her boss, the imposing Dr Kranstöver. As it was a smart restaurant, there was a live pianist sitting at a grand piano, playing the same sort of thing Jonathan had been listening to in the Kleines Haus. He tinkled away over the sound of the fountain the proprietors had installed on the terrace. How rare it was to be able to sit outside in Hamburg of an evening! And how reassuring that there were people in this world you got on with without even needing to talk much. Ulla clinked the glass stirrer in her cocktail. Suckling pig, as fresh as if it were alive, baked in wildflower honey pastry. She resolved to inspect Jonathan's room tomorrow morning – it was ages since she'd last read his diary. She would permit herself that treat.

Dr Kranstöver was looking forward to the exhibition, which was now all set to go – with or without Mexico – and kept saying he couldn't have managed it as well without Ulla. Their collaboration had been a success. Who would have thought it, back then, when she'd sat there in his office? Did she realize she had her ring to thank for this? The moment he saw it, he knew she was the one. He'd be leaving for the south of France in the next few days. He owned a delightful house near the Pyrenees, in the Béziers region where the Cathars were slaughtered; the mild wind drifted through it on bare feet, and once he got there he was going to let himself go. All the wonderful white bread they had down there, the beans and the splendid wine. And then he would embark on the final stage: writing the introductory essay for the exhibition on cruelty, his eighth great *oeuvre*.

Ah! France. A great people. So sensitive they deemed even linguistic inaccuracies 'cruel' – *les barbarismes*. We, on the other hand, we Germans were so coarse and uncivilized that in our part of the world the weather could be described as 'cruel'. In our culture this word – so important, so frightening – was trivialized and devalued. 'It's cruelly cold today . . .' The fact that it was possible to say this in German was pretty objection-able. It implied that one could also draw conclusions about other realms of feeling: our capacity for love, for example, which also clearly left a great deal to be desired. Love as the counterpart of cruelty.

Oh, to leave behind all the small irritations that made life so unpleasant here in the north. The journalists with their imbecilic critiques, the general public – all idiots these days – and the people from the town council who went through his expenses: why did he always take a taxi to the museum, and what about the big apartment in Rahlstedt? Was that really necessary when he had an attic apartment in the museum at his disposal?

Dr Kranstöver was working towards getting Ulla Bakkre de Vaera to accompany him to France. Perhaps his large Peugeot, which he would be fetching shortly to drive her home, would convince her to spend a few days with him there. First he would dangle the attic apartment – the penthouse, one might say – before her, tempt her with that. Then he would say: France. He pictured himself lying in a deckchair, surrounded by luxuriant shrubs, gazing at the mountains in the distance; he saw her emerge from the low, single-storey house, step over the mouldering threshold in a long skirt – barefoot, definitely – with a big, live fish in her hand, about to slaughter it with a sharp knife. He would – he must – make this vision a reality.

Ulla was thinking about a big fish too but in more concrete terms. Her part-time status had to change; that was what she was working towards. Twenty-nine years old and still not in regular employment! She eyed her boss over the rim of her slender-stemmed glass. He was peering through his half-moon spectacles and prodding at his trout, which stared up at him with boiled white eyes. She wondered whether, like Jonathan, he ever left dirty socks on his desk or yellowing earplugs moulded to the shape of his ear? He didn't have false teeth, she'd already established that much, so bad breath was unlikely.

And so she said that she wouldn't have thought it possible for him to design such a clear, compelling exhibition from the mass of material she had delivered. The courage of omission – the energy required to focus amorphous ideas and establish a dialogue between remote concepts! If they managed to get Mexico going as well, the outcome really could be described as artistic – the exhibition itself as a work of art – as it not only did justice to the individual exhibits but also consolidated them into a collage, transforming them into an overall statement of something entirely different. It was borderline genius the way he jumped back and forth to harness the profusion of material and convey a clear, humane insight: that injustice and cruelty should never be repeated in this world.

And so on and so forth.

This compliment put Dr Kranstöver in a cheerful mood, and he related where, when and how he had arranged the other seven exhibitions, counting them off on his fingers, exhibitions that had subsequently become sensations; and he declared that Meckel was an absolute clown, totally incompetent; this work would have been quite beyond him.

Meckel? asked Ulla. Then she remembered – thank God –

that this was a man in Bochum who was always causing trouble, and recalled why she ought to disapprove of him. Didn't he even have a speech impediment?

They got to the stewed fruit. Dr Kranstöver was of the opinion that cruelty was a particularly male domain, deriving perhaps from excessive strength or lack of occupation – a phenomenon that did not occur with women, as the normal woman was almost constantly occupied with childrearing and, sensitized by dealing with her brood, possessed a certain empathy.

'While the man sits by the fire whittling arrows, she suckles the boy . . .'

'Not always!' cried Ulla. It wasn't always like that; she could give examples to the contrary. That Cheka commissar – wasn't she called Dora? – in Minsk, and Ilse Koch, the Beast of Buchenwald: women. God forbid they ever be let loose! She thought that, when the worst came to the worst, men retained a scrap of fairness right to the end. Just think of female traffic wardens, those strangely uniformed hostesses who hunt down parking offenders. When those women gave out parking tickets you could shuffle about on your knees in front of them, but you'd be banging your head against a brick wall.

'But, Miss Ulla,' said Dr Kranstöver, seizing her hand at last, 'these women are notable exceptions – man-women, whose hormonal balance is disturbed.'

Ulla shook his hand as if in greeting. 'How would you know what a woman is capable of?' she said. She thought of Charlotte Corday, that painting by David of Marat lying dead in his bathtub.

Murder! she thought. Murder is not, in and of itself, an act of cruelty. The question is how it's done. She reflected that she might need to reorganize her card index after all. Girls in uniform, women against women – this was an aspect she hadn't yet considered. If she didn't, she might be accused of neglecting equal rights.

The rest of the evening was spent discussing secondary aspects of cruelty, specific outrages in the idyllic world of the upright citizen: dismissing pregnant women from their jobs, for example, or hit-and-run incidents, a male speciality, callously driving on and leaving someone injured in the road. It was a particularly repulsive manifestation of what outwardly respectable men were capable of.

Pedantry – wasn't that also a form of cruelty? said Dr Kranstöver. This was something to think about later. He thought excessive pedantry really was quite cruel as well, because it was aimed at the senses. Dotting the legal i's and crossing the t's when the whole panoply of life was on offer.

As he said this he was thinking about the attic apartment in the museum with its view over the roofs of Hamburg. He resolved to offer it to this young woman the following morning.

8

Jonathan presented himself punctually at the airport in his coat and spotted bow-tie. He paid the taxi driver and entered the airport building, which bristled with antennae.

The automatic doors slid obsequiously aside, and warm air, tinted with music, billowed towards him. Indicator boards rattled out updates on delays. Jonathan strolled through the bright hall, unimpressed by the utopian airs of those trying to book cheap holidays to Tunisia, people dressed for leisure activities, with children called Denis and Jacqueline.

A Turkish man drove past at a leisurely speed in a special vehicle, polishing the floor. He was singing quietly to himself. This, thought Jonathan, must be far more pleasant than tilling a field in the wastes of Anatolia. Nozzles at the front of the machine squirted white emulsion, erasing the dirt that was tracked in from every corner of the world on the soles of people's shoes. The last surviving insects ran for their lives.

Jonathan exchanged ten five-mark notes at the bank, as advised. He bought some newspapers at a kiosk, and beside him stood the footballer Manni Koch, the man who missed the penalty in the last European Cup, looking for razor blades. That made his day. Bumping into this man made the whole trip worthwhile.

In the airport restaurant Jonathan met up with the Santubara Company crew, Frau Winkelvoss and Hansi Strohtmeyer, as arranged. They'd just been thinking: Oh, for God's sake, this writer isn't going to make it; he probably reckons it's not until tomorrow, or he flew out yesterday, despite '9.30 a.m. airport restaurant' being highlighted with red marker pen on the paper . . . They leapt up and offered him their chairs, even though there were two free chairs at the table. Perhaps they were even a little disappointed that he'd actually turned up; it was hard to say.

Frau Winkelvoss was small and radiant. (Jonathan straightened his bow-tie when he saw her.) She was swathed in a frilly blouse and scented scarves, which she had teamed with gold-buckled Russian-leather mercenary boots.

'Did you order this lovely weather?'

Hansi Strohtmeyer, the powerfully built chauffeur, stood beside her, looking almost shy. Actually, he wasn't a chauffeur at all – Frau Winkelvoss was amused that Jonathan had been under this impression – but a highly paid test and racing driver. He had been involved in three very serious accidents and was still incredibly fit. He'd been on that super-rally in the Sahara, the one where eighteen people died – lorries, motorcycles, small cars, all piled up – driving past camel caravans over sand dunes shaped by the wind, being filmed from a helicopter. He'd also been stranded in a river in South America.

The two of them were eating smoked salmon, which had

been fattened on vitamin mash in Norway, and talking about their boss, who had dreamt up and organized the East Prussia thing. He sent his regards. He'd asked them to tell Jonathan to find an unusual angle when writing about the Poland trip, and had given them an envelope for him containing an advance of five hundred marks, which demonstrated a good understanding of the realities of life. Writers, as everyone knows, never have any money.

Jonathan ordered a pie. Frau Winkelvoss, who he noticed was wearing an agreeable perfume, gave him a Santubara folder containing brochures, maps, the plane ticket 'and so on and so forth' and his passport with the visa stamped in it. Although she said it was touching how nice the Poles were – kind, hospitable, vivacious – there was something or other she wanted to impress on him, and he mustn't, for heaven's sake, do this or that in 'Gdańsk'. And he mustn't lose his passport or all hell would break loose. It was immediately apparent that they thought him a likeable loser and would have preferred to hang the ticket around his neck as if he were embarking on the Children's Evacuation Programme.

Frau Winkelvoss, whose first name was Anita, said she thought they'd have to keep a bit of an eye on him. She even wagged a warning finger.

And so they were off to Poland – to East Prussia, the 'German regions'. The three of them were looking forward to the tour: it was quite special, because who went to East Prussia these days? They were curious to discover what there was to see there. Polish women were said to be stunningly attractive, but after three years they started losing their figure.

'They have no idea Germans used to live there.'

Should he buy anything else? Cigarettes? Sticking plasters? Would they be cast adrift over the border?

No, there was no need. The Santubara people knew of special shops in Orbis hotels where Western currency bought you anything your heart desired. Besides, Poles weren't born yesterday. In the past the two of them had purchased all sorts of things on the black market – bread, butter, sausages, a mountain of stuff for the equivalent of one mark seventy-five; they'd sat in a ditch by the roadside and scoffed the lot.

Don't forget to bring back some Krakauer smoked sausages. You won't find a sausage like it anywhere in Europe!

Naturally they had arrived too early. They had to wait an hour and a half. Another beer, and another.

See that weird family at the nearby table, with the mentally handicapped child who was drooling? Were they planning on taking him with them somewhere when he couldn't control his face and wore a leather helmet to prevent him from injuring himself? What must that cost? they wondered. Imagine – and people in India have nothing to eat!

Cream of tomato soup, sirloin tips, cold cuts on a wooden plate. Frau Winkelvoss, small as she was, consumed a whole mountain of yellow, brown and green ice cream; it had a little paper parasol on top that she licked clean and slipped in her handbag. She burped charmingly, and went on talking about 'Gdańsk' – what one had to keep an eye out for there, meaning what Jonathan needed to find an unusual angle for, and what she had to keep an eye out for herself.

Adios, Madonna.
  It was a beautiful time!
Adios, Madonna.
  You're no longer mine . . .
I see you so happy to be in his arms,
And now I miss you so,
Adios, Madonna!
  I was a fool to let you go!

Frau Winkelvoss pushed up her bracelets and lit a cigarillo. She made one last call to Mutzbach, during which she informed them that she had seen the footballer Manni Koch in the cafeteria, the poor lad who had missed the penalty; she'd never have guessed he was so small. How was he supposed to stand up to the big guys? Of course, she also passed on the fact that Jonathan Fabrizius, the oddball writer, had thought Hansi Strohtmeyer was the chauffeur. This was now doing the rounds in Mutzbach.

Jonathan made one last attempt to reach his girlfriend. Their goodbyes had been brief. She wasn't at home, and he couldn't disturb her at the museum; she was probably looking through the collection of paintings from the States with Dr Kranstöver. Images of executions in the electric chair, which – believe it or not – lasted up to ten minutes. The painters of these pictures had taken Otto Dix's shell-shocked 'shakers' as their inspiration.

Frau Winkelvoss made another quick visit to 'the little girls' room', and Jonathan bought a pack of ten miniature bottles of Eau de Cologne. Then the small group headed to Gate 39, where they had to wait another half an hour.

It was an odd feeling for her, said Frau Winkelvoss, being escorted by two such handsome men, one on either side.

In the search cubicle, Jonathan spread his coat before the policeman like an exhibitionist and thanked the man for doing his job, commenting that it must be incredibly boring. (He didn't ask whether he'd ever caught anyone; he assumed the policeman must be sick to death of that question.) He tried to spot his bag on the monitor, to see what it looked like in its defamiliarized state. As always when he went abroad, Jonathan regarded the German passport officers with a degree of wistfulness. Soon he would be placing himself under foreign sovereignty, a guest; he would have to hold his tongue instead of being allowed to demonstrate his superiority. When you'd started a world war, murdered Jews and taken people's bicycles away (in Holland) the cards were stacked against you. Why had he let himself in for this? Could he still turn back?

Jonathan moved away from his colleagues and sat down with his back to the panoramic window so he could people-watch undisturbed. These people, in turn, wanted to watch the jets rolling past on the runway, and those funny airport vehicles, very small but incredibly wide, as they zipped about and bustled back and forth, and the border guards' tank roasting in the sun. The people waiting here for the flight to Danzig looked different from the utopian figures in the main terminal building: not very elegant, more rustic – a bit like Russian *matkas* flying from Tbilisi to Moscow to sell two kilos of strawberries. They looked outlandish – the English word 'strange' came to Jonathan's mind. There was a Polish child, a huge pink teddy bear under its arm with a voice box that sang 'Happy Birthday to You'. A man in white leather shoes. A woman in a red hat. Had she been a Canadian tourist wearing it in Munich she wouldn't have stood out, but here, in this serious environment, it looked odd, even silly. His attention was caught by an old woman dressed entirely in black. Perhaps during the war she'd had to go into hiding? Or had kept a German woman as a slave after the war? Or was she a German going to look at her parents' estate, where they'd kept Russian prisoners of war in a wooden crate?

All the Poles travelling back to their homeland had something in their luggage that they weren't allowed to bring with them. In Hamburg they'd been assertive; after all, the Germans had wrecked their country and still hadn't paid any reparations. Now, with the imminent prospect of encountering the Polish airport police, they came across as simpler, more pious, than they probably were.

The LOT aeroplane was parked at the perimeter of the airport as if in quarantine. It had an unfamiliar look to it: it wasn't a Boeing but a Russian make, similar to a Boeing but distinctly different too. It lacked that finishing touch – Western design, or whatever you'd call it: the fuselage looked too short compared to the tail, and there was a bulge like a double chin under the cockpit. And the seats inside weren't numbered, so people immediately started pushing and shoving. 'Sometimes you'll even see chickens sitting in the gangway,' he'd been told.

Jonathan shoved his coat into the overhead locker, five-mark coins raining down on him as he did so, and squeezed himself into his seat.

'These seats are for pygmies!'

The people behind him were digging their knees into his back, and a miasma of garlic wafted from the row in front. A Caucasian-looking fellow with silver teeth sat down beside him, the type who slaughters lambs by slitting their throats and letting them bleed to death. He wore a black Persian hat and had a shapeless bag on his lap, and couldn't believe Jonathan had taken the window seat. There was no parleying with this magnificent specimen, whose favourite dish was possibly rancid butter; armrest hostilities were initiated immediately. Hansi Strohtmeyer and Frau Winkelvoss were sitting further forward, near the emergency exit – 'the predetermined breaking point', the racing-car driver jested. When Jonathan got up to nip to the toilet before take-off, Strohtmeyer called after him, 'We're not there yet!'

Peace descended as they flew over the Baltic Sea. The civilized west sank away, the barbarous east approached. Jonathan thought about the red-brick churches, his northern goddesses, their chests still facing proudly westwards to this day, as they had for centuries. The old slogan popped into his head – 'The Baltic Sea is the Ocean of Peace' – and he imagined ships symbolizing the brotherhood between peoples flying colourful pennants and transporting singing workers from here to there and from there to here amid shouts of *Druzhba!*; pork cutlets with *pommes frites*, humanitarian rockets at night accompanied by guitars and songs about the people, who basically wanted nothing to do with war; ploughing through the clayey water, lone submarines lurking in its depths that might quietly, quietly, quietly be creeping towards the skerries of Sweden, land of peace – raise the periscope for a moment, quickly snap it down again – settling into a crevice in the rock where it has no business; open a hatch to release tiny amphibious tanks, lay down depots just in case . . .

'When we have Sweden, Finland will fall into our lap all by itself.'

At this very moment freighters were embarking from the Scandinavian land of peace, their mysterious cargoes shrouded in brown sailcloth: howitzers with extra-penetrating power, landmines with delayed-action fuses and small rockets any schoolchild could fire, capable of bringing down jumbo jets full of tourists and business people out of the sky. Military equipment bound for allied, peace-loving countries, to help them defend themselves against class enemies attacking them with similar weapons, against states of an imperialist nature that sought to seize, exploit or subjugate them. Jonathan thought of how, at the site of a plane crash, photo-journalists always managed to find a doll with its arms torn off to splash across the front page, and how the headlines always said SEVEN PEOPLE ARE STILL MISSING and you never heard whether they eventually turned up after all – sitting in a pub, maybe, having a beer to celebrate their survival, or blundering through the reeds, shirt flapping, with only one shoe. In glossy magazines you saw tattered dolls with big, questioning, blinking eyes, not crushed human heads, because the dolls were a way of skipping sublimely over the ghastliness. Pictures of crushed heads and ripped-off hands were deposited in depots. Jonathan wondered whether one day he might use his press card to gain access to these depots on some pretext or other and write a feature on 'The Pictures They Withhold from Us'.

Jonathan stared down at the choppy, greenish-grey sea. He imagined how difficult it must be to paddle across this large expanse of water in a canoe at night with your child in front and your wife behind. Escape! Is the pension certificate in the dry-bag? And then an article in the local paper in

Gedser: '. . . fished out of the icy water, utterly exhausted . . .'

And then the officials in Schleswig-Holstein, who could only be described as Western cretins or Western cows, sitting there behind their vacuum flasks. 'Why did you take the risk? All that glitters isn't gold here in the West either, you know! What in heaven's name were you thinking?' You might be prosecuted too, because of the child, whose life had recklessly been endangered: we live in a constitutional state, after all.

Jonathan imagined that other escape too, in 1945: the great creaking steamships laden right up to the promenade deck with refugees, people piled up in the mahogany dining room like sardines, pea soup and dry bread, the women in headscarves, the little boys in balaclavas: only one suitcase per person; please leave prams on the shore.

Must I then? Must I then? From the town must I then?

Leave the horse-drawn carts on the quay as well, loaded with boxes and trunks, items such as wooden bowls for kneading sausage meat, household goods painstakingly hauled over icebound roads; leave it all behind, the chest of drawers and the grandfather clock too. But take the little briefcase with the jewellery, Grandfather's gold watch, amethysts and emeralds that might not even be real.

'We'll take care of the horses,' the soldiers say.

It hurts, though, to leave the two chestnuts behind; they've lowered their heads; it feels like a betrayal. They realize they're being deserted. And the land of the fathers, along the river? That was good soil. They let the pigs and cows on to the threshing floor and scattered feed there for them.

Jonathan remembered the Soviet submarine that had picked out the biggest refugee ship. Fire! cried the Russian commander, and there was a thump, and the ship, with its promenade deck, swimming pool and mahogany dining room, keeled over on to its side; the dishes slid to the floor, and the cutlery, and no one played hymns.

Nearer, my God, to Thee!

It was eighteen degrees below zero. People jumped into the water and were crushed by ice floes. Severed legs, severed heads. And for this heroic deed the Soviet submarine commander received a medal, and today, feeding pigeons in Leningrad, he's still pleased with himself for doing such a good job. Treasure hunters with robots don't bother with this wreck; they'd find nothing but bones on the seabed, fifty-five metres down. At best a briefcase with Grandfather's gold watch, emeralds and amethysts that might not even be real. No gold bars, no Amber Room, nothing for them to bring up but bones; any investment would be a complete waste of money.

Strange, thought Jonathan, that no one fixes a buoy above the wreck: IN MEMORY OF THE 5,438 PEOPLE WHO DIED HERE. Surely it could be done, technically speaking? You have to let things go, he thought, or life would be unendurable. And he pictured his uncle carrying his dead mother into the church, this woman who had breathed her last, who had not even been included in the statistics, who lived on only as a snapshot.

Jonathan gazed down at the Ocean of Peace. What a pity, he thought, that they don't announce whether that's still Mecklenburg down there, or 'Poland' already. There was a town – probably 'Szczecin' on the 'Odra', or perhaps 'Kohlwietze' or whatever Kolberg was called these days. A town with a northern goddess enthroned at its centre, which must be brought up out of the depths and into the light for the enjoyment of mankind. It was indescernible right now on account of the poisonous clouds being pumped into the air from the ground. 'Szczecin' – there'd been no mention of that at Yalta. The Poles had slipped it in their pocket; it was actually on this side of the Oder. Perhaps this would come back to haunt them one day? Perhaps one day suitcases would have to be packed there again and everything cleared out 'within the hour'?

He could see a river too, getting wider and wider, washing yellowish sludge out to sea.

Now the stewardesses brought a snack, which was up to Western standards: sandwiches wrapped in cellophane and even a bar of chocolate. Jonathan pocketed the chocolate. He'd give the chocolate to Polish children. The coffee tasted slightly odd. As for the stewardesses, they could not be described as stunningly attractive: they seemed to have skipped the Aphrodite phase of their development and lost their figure straight away.

Two rows ahead of him Frau Winkelvoss pocketed the chocolate as well. Flowery packaging! She would take it back for her boss to show him how touchingly backward they were here. She was having quite a lively conversation with Hansi Strohtmeyer about the head of department who'd dreamt up this PR trip to the east: state-of-the-art V8 engines against a backdrop of dilapidated towns. He was quite a forceful person, who had good qualities too. She repeated what they needed to do first when they got to Gdańsk, and that they mustn't forget anything, for heaven's sake. Herr Strohtmeyer wanted to know whether she'd seen the footballer Manni Koch? The bloke who'd missed the penalty? He'd met him in the loos, looked like a perfectly normal bloke.

Now Frau Winkelvoss turned round and mouthed a question to Jonathan: Everything OK?

Yes, everything OK, Jonathan gesticulated back. It'll all work out!

The Caucasian guy beside him spurned the modern cellophane-wrapped LOT food. He brought out a sausage and a loaf of bread and cut himself a slice against his thumb with his pocket knife.

9

Danzig: first Polish, then German, then Free City, then German again and Polish again. The airport in Danzig was a hut with GDAŃSK painted on it, with no jets rolling past or grotesquely shaped, eager little cars.

It's as if Bad Zwischenahn had an airport, thought Jonathan. And Hansi Strohtmeyer said, 'So what do they do here in winter?'

One people, one Reich, one Führer! Hitler, wearing an aviator hat, steps out of his Ju 52, riding crop in hand, and schoolchildren everywhere write an essay: 'The Führer Over Germany'.

To the planes, to the planes!
Comrade, there's no turning back!

Parachutes slip from the body of the aeroplane, one after another, and the parachutists float to the ground, penknives in the side pockets of their trousers. On Crete, farmers gouged out the eyes of the wounded.

The woman with the red hat and the child with the pink teddy bear, an incredibly naughty boy. The gruff Polish language

– this must have been how German sounded to the French back then, in 1940. The old woman in black was met at the airport by a Russian limousine and whisked past all the checkpoints; the chauffeur removed his cap as she stepped in.

The luggage took a long time. One man delivered it by hand, pulling the rusty carts along by himself. It made you want to go and help. Sitting in the lounge was like being in a cinema; there was a lot of plywood and linoleum, and you could see the officials at the front nosing about in people's suitcases, spending longer on the women's than the men's. The delegation from Hamburg last, please. The young officials in the plywood cabins checked every page of the passports – what? New York? – wrote down how much money these crazy foreigners were bringing in and made a note of cameras, serial numbers and so on, to prevent them being flogged in Poland or possibly exchanged for valuable goods, thereby disturbing the carefully preserved socialist balance: amber for pocket calculators, for example, or silver foxes that would go to the opera in Frankfurt.

And sausages.

The Santubara group was last. They were asked whether they wanted some fuel vouchers. Frau Winkelvoss thought this was marvellous. Nothing against fuel vouchers; at least that way no one could steal their money, and perhaps with these vouchers you got to jump the queue at petrol stations? She bought enough coupons to fuel a round-the-world trip, despite Hansi Strohtmeyer repeatedly signalling to her to stop.

It was a mystery why they didn't introduce these petrol coupons in Germany, said Frau Winkelvoss. That way you could provide workers with cheaper petrol and make factory owners and fat cats pay through the nose. Petrol coupons in different colours, then use them somehow to regulate environmental pollution. Each individual Pole was allowed only thirty litres of petrol a month, which was brilliant; they probably didn't need more or they'd surely get it.

She whispered conspiratorially, first in Hansi Strohtmeyer's ear and then in Jonathan's, about the black-market rate she'd managed to get that summer: a thousand zlotys for ten marks. Hansi talked about how you could exchange money at good rates in Morocco too, but the notes were sometimes forgeries. He followed up with a Helmut Kohl joke featuring an electric chair that failed to do its job.

He had some Polish jokes as well. '"What's in this shop, my good man?" "No shirts. You'll find no shoes next door."'

An hour later Frau Winkelvoss said that they sometimes took a very long time to process people in Hamburg too; and she'd once spent a whole night at the airport in Turkey. In Egypt people were incredibly friendly. But the Arabs in Abu Dhabi, when she was on a stopover there, had given her the creeps. Like characters from the *Arabian Nights*.

Hansi Strohtmeyer was playing with a matchbox, throwing it up in the air and catching it. When he got bored he took out a match, split it and used it to pick his teeth.

After another half an hour Frau Winkelvoss said, 'The Poles simply can't organize a thing. I love it.' She'd taken off her shoes and was doing toe exercises. Jonathan looked at her small firm feet.

Outside, young people wanting to exchange money waited for them as if they were rich uncles from America; they begged for cigarettes and asked for pocket calculators. A Polish travel expert with a badge on his lapel had also appeared, sent by the Ministry of Tourism to welcome the little crew. It was whispered that this man had once been a general and that he had quite a history – he'd been a general, then he'd done time for something or other, then been released, and now here he was in tourism.

In the car park stood two fabulous Santubara V8s with extra-wide tyres. They'd been driven across East Germany, and now here they were, washed and cleaned, bang on time. The technicians who came with the cars greeted the racing hero Hansi Strohtmeyer and the comical little woman Anita Winkelvoss, then eyed Jonathan curiously. So this was the man who'd mistaken the great Hansi Strohtmeyer for a chauffeur!

Strohtmeyer selected one of the two supercars. The technicians would accompany them in the other in case anything should happen.

The Polish general drove on ahead in a Lada, and the Santubara crew followed in their supercars like members of the master race. You didn't need to drive fast in these. Jonathan was curious as to what he was about to experience and glad that he'd agreed to come on this well-prepared adventure. He thought of those excessively long American cars, the black Lincoln thingies that pull up outside the Waldorf Astoria and a solitary woman gets out with a white toy poodle under her arm, and all she wants is to buy a box of chocolates.

In this way they crawled along not to Danzig but to Gdingen, with all the Lada people looking round to see whether there was something wrong for them to be crawling along like that. The tourism general was very sorry that there hadn't been a single room to be found in Danzig, even though they'd made the booking months ago. There was a Western-standard hotel with a bar and all the trimmings but no vacancies.

They saw several cars in the ditch and others being pushed. People pushing cars together? Frau Winkelvoss thought it was fantastic the way they helped each other out here. You didn't get that in the West! They wouldn't have to push the Santubara, obviously. Like all new cars it smelt faintly of rotten egg-whites; but the digital display on the dashboard was tippety-top, the miniature screen that showed everything was fine, no lights on anywhere that shouldn't be, no doors open – and ding-dong, all hell's bells went off if you did anything wrong.

It would not have occurred to Jonathan to refer to Gdingen, a city conjured out of thin air after the Great War, as 'Gotenhafen', the name it was given in September 1939.

The foyer of the Western-standard hotel was sumptuously decorated with artificial flowers and crammed with massive fake-leather armchairs. A wave of paralytic Scandinavians rolled towards them; they'd come here specially from their squeaky-clean country to get tanked up on the cheap.

The hotel was pretty comfortable although, as the wheezing tourism general informed them, the swimming pool was closed at night and you had to hand over your passport when you went to bed. You can put up with stuff like that, even if sensitive people do see it as a sort of emasculation and it can prompt outbursts of fury from those who have a short fuse. Hansi Strohtmeyer had had very different experiences in the Sahara. Did they give you fifty thousand zlotys for ten pfennigs here, he wanted to know.

'It's pronounced "zwotty",' said Frau Winkelvoss. She found

the Polish banknotes 'kinda great'. She also found it 'kinda quaint' that they had to wait two hours to place a long-distance call, not like in bloody West Germany where everything works and you're harried from pillar to post. Here you couldn't call Germany directly, it had to go via the telephone exchange, but it could be worse; after all, they'd only just come from there.

'It'll be fine.'

The general said goodbye and wished the crew all the best. If they needed anything, all they had to do was call him. He was shocked to discover that the Santubara Company's annual turnover was considerably larger than the gross national product of the whole of Poland. So all that socialist drudgery had been in vain, as had the protest that had cost him six years, and acting as an informer, as he was now obliged to do.

A porter, who – as he put it – didn't really know whether he was a German or a Pole, led the group over to the lift. It had a grille of wrought-iron garlands and juddered from floor to floor. They were in three rooms directly above each other (on account of the bugging system). The ride in the lift gave them the opportunity to learn that the exchange rate here was one mark to one hundred and fifty zlotys, and you could hike it up to one mark to three hundred and sixty zlotys if you were determined. All wonderful, and so terribly charming.

The rooms were perfectly normal rooms. You got frayed armchair upholstery in Frankfurt too, and hotel curtains are revolting all over the world. There was even a bar of soap in the toilet and green shampoo that smelt of tar in a little plastic pillow.

The hand towels had a slightly rancid odour, but at least the television had two channels on offer, which was enough, after all – although it was funny that the people in *Dallas* spoke Polish here. And everything in black and white! Actually, though, black and white was kind of progressive. We've had it up to here with 'colour'.

Jonathan went over to the window. Down below men were loitering in the car park, tampering with parked cars when the parking attendants weren't looking. They didn't dare approach the two V8s with their double-injection engines; one of the two technicians was standing there holding a pair of pliers.

A traditional sailing ship lay in the roads; a little further out was a warship, which, if Jonathan wasn't very much mistaken, was the peace warship from Hamburg. Jonathan thought about the Westerplatte peninsula. His uncle had talked about German soldiers who were still hiding in a bunker there ten years after the war ended, living on their provisions, finally staggering out into the open like axolotls.

It occurred to Jonathan that his uncle looked like Julius Streicher, the publisher of the anti-Semitic Nazi tabloid *Der Stürmer*. How peculiar . . . right down to his moustache and riding breeches.

But he was a thoroughly good man.

'We'll meet at three o'clock, then,' they'd said. After he had 'freshened up', as Frau Winkelvoss put it, Jonathan took the lift downstairs. In the foyer he exchanged two five-mark coins with an inexperienced man for an insane quantity of zlotys. The man extracted each note individually from his trouser pocket, scrunched up in a ball, and suddenly Jonathan was a kind of

Croesus. When the others arrived they said, 'What? You've exchanged money already?' And: Five-mark coins? They hadn't thought of that. Even though they'd been to Egypt and Morocco and eaten watermelon in Mali for Five pfennigs a slice, this had not occurred to them. So Herr Fabrizius wasn't that removed from everyday life after all! The receptionists behind the desk were whispering and pointing at him, but this had nothing to do with the illegal financial transaction; it was on account of his bow-tie, which they found comical. Better get in the back and write that down straight away; it'd go down well in the article.

The technicians handed over one of the cars to Hansi Stroht-meyer, and the man, whose name was Herr Schütte, explained to him the digital display on the dashboard, the tiny screen with symbols for seat belts, doors and headlamps, and the little integrated computer: how long you'd been driving, how many kilometres, how many kilometres per litre and so on, not for-getting average consumption.

In the car, which had been washed yet again, they drove along an avenue into Danzig. On the left was the Lenin Ship-yard – 'We'll take a look at that crazy Solidarność monument too; maybe that's something for the cultural programme?' – and, on the right, *Gründerzeit* villas, which had presumably been homes for coal merchants or even shipowners. 'What? Refugees?' said the shipowner's wife in February 1945. 'No, we can't take them in.' And three days later they were forced to hobble westwards themselves. As they rolled past the villas, overtaking crowded trams and lorries with lopsided cargo beds, the computer registered everything worth knowing – facts you didn't actually need to know, but which had a calming effect.

*

SOPOT, Jonathan read on a road sign. A picture of 'Zoppot' from his geography textbook flashed through his mind: a beach pavilion with a jazz band. If he were a Pole, and if he'd had any say at all in what happened back in the year of patriotic victory, he would have distorted the German place names beyond all recognition. Sopot? Anyone could tell it had once been called Zoppot. He would have called the place Klatschi, or . . . what was 'sunshine' in Polish? He would have started with that somehow. Sopot: it was too unimaginative. Jonathan found it disappointing.

The Marienkirche rose up unexpectedly over the roofs. There she was, the northern goddess, more delicate than expected; graceful, not bulky. Number seven in Jonathan's collection of churches. And then, in an instant, she was gone.

Where, he wondered, was the Polish Post Office in which the brave Polish postal workers had died? That must be around here somewhere. And the street Hitler drove down? Flowers, flowers, flowers. We welcome our Führer. *Sieg Heil!*

They bypassed the Old Town, with the Marienkirche and her lovely sisters, and parked in front of the Orbis Hotel; the technicians' vehicle had already arrived. You could buy whisky here, and men's heads carved out of gnarled lumps of wood. It was reasonable to assume that there would also be Krakauer sausages.

They split up, as they each had their own idea of what constituted a stroll around town and there was no point in following one another around the whole time.

Frau Winkelvoss instructed Jonathan to do a nice write-up of everything that crossed his path. She went to the phone to pick a bone with the asthmatic general from the Ministry of Tourism, as certain things had been promised to her that had not materialized.

Strohtmeyer had already disappeared.

Wasn't the Gauleiter of Danzig called Forster?

Jonathan went straight to the Marienkirche. If he was arrested and deported by the police on account of the illegal zlotys or his German-language map, at least he wouldn't have missed northern goddess no. 7. They would have done better to finish it off with one big tower instead of all the little ones, Jonathan thought, circling the old red walls. A mason was hanging from the top of the roof ridge, pasting over some cracks.

Then he went into the house of prayer, mingling with the sailors and the schoolchildren, the housewives and the German homeland association people; he walked around it three times, at first with his head tilted right back, the way strangers do in New York, then glancing to the left and right to see if there was something magnificent waiting to be discovered.

'Look, Mummy, that's where the astronomical clock used to be!' he heard a seventy-year-old woman say to a decrepit old lady, supporting her with a firm grip under the arm. The two women were with the homeland association group; the old lady had wanted to see the walls of her home town once more (inexpensively) and then die. She hadn't thought she'd ever get there again.

Jonathan took snaps of the whitewashed arches with his pocket camera. It ought to be open at the top, he felt: a glass roof. Even then, though, it would still be closed. The way to heaven is closed, he thought. He had similar ideas standing in front of the Memling painting, *The Last Judgement*, that elliptical circuit of good and evil. The archangel in the middle with the scales in his hand, and, up above, the intercessors to the left and right of the triune God. The intercessors on the left, thought Jonathan, when do they pack up and go over to the other side? They need to do it in good time, otherwise they'll plunge with the damned into the maw of hell. He also pondered the picture's strange history: destined for Holland, captured at sea and brought to Danzig, stolen by Napoleon and brought to Paris, then transported back again on a lumbering horse and cart. How many paintings had gone missing during daring actions like these? The Reformation, the Iconoclastic Fury: altars hacked to pieces and thrown into the flames. Perhaps the greatest art was long gone, and we were making do with pale imitations? What sort of people must they have been to hack Gothic and Romanesque altars to pieces? Medieval SA men, probably. Depictions of hell: something else for his girlfriend in Hamburg. Had she thought of it already?

Jonathan bought a four-colour print of the Memling for Ulla. He also photographed everything two or three times, just in case. Unfortunately there was no 'literature' at the entrance from which to discover how high, how wide, how old his goddess was. He was, however, able to find a guide who informed him that the Marienkirche was the biggest brick-built church in the world: 105 metres long, sixty-six metres wide, with a surface area of 4,115 square metres and room for twenty-four thousand people. The homeland association group certainly didn't stand out in this vast space. They were huddled in a corner, debating whether they might dare to sing a song here, something from the old days. 'Take Thou My

Hand, O Father' – surely that would be quite innocuous. Best not, though; they might break the laboriously knotted threads of rapprochement. Best to wait a bit longer with a thing like that.

On the way out Jonathan sacrificed a thousand-zloty note – he had made one last circuit specifically in order to determine whether that was a lot of money or a little. Twenty-seven marks fifty, he had worked out; but, as he realized outside, this was, unfortunately, a miscalculation. Then he strolled through the reconstructed streets. There was something not quite right about the restored city. The houses looked just like the old photographs, absolutely correct, but it was as if they were standing on the seabed, like the houses in Vineta. Nor did it help that they'd shot the television adaptation of *Buddenbrooks* here.

When Jonathan stopped to look at jewellery in the window of a souvenir shop near the Green Gate, an impeccably restored Renaissance structure, the gypsy women surged forward, one quite old with big gaps in her teeth, one younger and one adolescent girl. These three outlandish individuals probably lived off hedgehogs baked in clay on an open fire. They made a beeline for him and pressed him hard – 'Chair-mun? Oh! Chairmunny is beeyootiful country . . .' – and wanted to show him a trick; he liked a bit of fun, didn't he? He was to give them his wallet to hold, just for a moment, and in a few seconds it would have more money in it than before. This was the trick they wanted to show him, if he knew how to have fun, and they assumed he did, because he looked so funny in his pretty bow-tie, and was Chair-mun, as well . . .

Jonathan shrank back. He leapt into the souvenir shop,

where he was safe for the time being. Through the shop window he watched the women take up positions a short distance away, ready to intercept him when he re-emerged. There were several of these female money-multiplication troops about; the Polish police observed them but didn't stop them plying their trade. Didn't they know that foreigners were being pestered here? What kind of impression did that make?

Jonathan sat down with the friendly proprietor, who laid out antique amber jewellery in front of him and praised it insincerely. He didn't want to name prices up front; they could do that later. The objects in question were fist-sized lumps of milky amber set in silver, necklaces of polished oval pearls that got bigger and bigger, and all manner of brooches. 'Never mind the price, we'll work that out. We'll come to an agreement, don't worry.' He didn't have any of those Polish wooden figurines, but if Jonathan gave him some money he could get hold of them.

The proprietor spoke good German. He'd just been to Hamburg, he said; he had a branch there. A friend of his came in, and naturally they spoke to each other in Polish – about old watches from the Nazi era, perhaps, square things with luminous dials, or silver that the Germans had stolen from the Jews and then had to leave behind. Jonathan sat in the corner, almost unheeded, taking it all in. He made a mental note of a few things for which he would later find an unusual angle, as had been drummed into him by the Santubara people. A small boy brought a pot of coffee and biscuits, and Jonathan was offered some too. Tourists came in and had the mickey taken out of them; there were time-wasters who just wanted to look around a bit and foreign men with gold teeth and wads of notes in their pockets. Jonathan would not have been surprised if Albert Schindeloe had shown up.

Finally, a decrepit man entered the shop. He let first the owner and then Jonathan peer into his shopping bag, which had books in it.

Jonathan took one out. It was in German, entitled:

The Typewriter
and the History of Its Development

– a small-format book with lots of illustrations. Inside the cover was a purple stamp:

HERMANN BINDER

KRAKAU

ADOLF-HITLER-PLATZ 5

Jonathan felt this was worthy of note and bought it for a handful of zlotys.

He would, of course, have liked to buy the lump of milky amber, but he didn't have three hundred and sixty marks, which is what it turned out he would have to pay for it. Anyway, how would he have got the thing across the border? And for that price he could buy something similar in Hamburg.

To purchase his liberty, he picked out a little brooch instead, put a few zloty notes on the table and left the shop.

Outside, the three women pounced on him, wanting to show him the money trick they had promised. He kept them at bay by crossing himself, even though he wasn't a Catholic. It was a spontaneous action, and it had an immediate effect. The women shrank back; one of them cried, 'Bastard!' and they reconvened a little way off. Never had they experienced such a thing. So now he was a German swine, and a crafty one at that.

Jonathan strolled a while longer past the rows of reconstructed houses, up on the left, down on the right, past people queueing for fish and sugar, approaching sparse groups of tourists. 'Yes, that's it! Exactly!' cried former Danzig residents, praising the ersatz architecture of the old alleyways; that lion, which an official restorer was in the process of scrubbing clean again – wonderful! We used to ride on it when we were children. Well, on the statue that was there before, which looked exactly the same. Must take a photo, send it home to show our sons, who strangely can't muster any enthusiasm for the old homeland.

They haven't been able to resurrect the corpse, only transform it, Jonathan thought, into a figure that belongs in a waxworks exhibition. And what a shame you can't reconstruct human beings: the figures of the saved whom Memling sent to heaven, for example, or the ones in the jaws of hell, the fallen. Bring the damned and the blessed back to life and lead them naked through the alleyways with ropes around their necks, signal to them – it'll be all right – and get a signal from them of what it's like over there. But they're not allowed to speak.

At the Artus Court he was stopped by an elderly woman. She looked German, but she definitely wasn't from Germany. She looked like a friendly pub landlady, and Jonathan didn't for one moment think she was about to beg from him. The woman had an empty medicine bottle in her hand; she told him her daughter was sick and she couldn't get this medicine anywhere in Poland. Might Jonathan get it for her and send it when he returned to Germany?

Jonathan looked at his watch. It was half past four, and he wanted a coffee, so he asked the woman where she lived. Perhaps they could go there, drink a coffee and discuss it?

The woman hesitated for a moment; then she put the little bottle in her pocket, said, 'Please, follow me,' and marched off. Jonathan walked behind her, looking at her thin legs, the darned grey stockings, and thinking that his mother would now be about the same age as this woman. This morning he had been sitting in the Isestrasse eating a couple of bread rolls with honey. Now he was having an adventure, the kind that would make a good story later on.

10

The woman's name was Kuschinski. She lived in an old building, its gable adorned with stucco tendrils and a date, triumphantly displayed. The wall above the facade was peppered with holes from machine-gun fire. Washing hung from windows embellished with decorative columns.

The lift, which had a wrought-iron grille and had once been very grand, was nailed up with planks of wood. They climbed the stairs – the walls of the stairwell were tiled – to an apartment door with a padlock and a long row of nameplates. Someone was chopping wood down in the basement.

A blast of stale air billowed out at Jonathan as the woman opened the door. Three families and assorted subtenants lived in the apartment. The room she took him to – he ducked on entering – had been crudely divided off, as you could see from the stucco ceiling; a small grey room with the lights on. It was crammed full of department store furniture: a wall unit with matching table (doily, vase), television (doily, wooden deer), fridge (doily, glass bowl) and a tiny glass prism lamp hanging from the ceiling. In the corner stood a basket full of laundry.

A gilt-framed picture hung on the wall, and under the

window was a flowered sofa with bedding on it from which someone had just emerged: the sick daughter.

Jonathan took it all in in one go. It seared itself on his retinal memory. He sat down in one of the flowered armchairs, fiddled with his bow-tie and thought: I'm just going to sit here for a while. He felt as if he belonged. The bedding on the sofa . . . When he'd had mumps his uncle had let him lie in his office. If Hansi Strohtmeyer were looking for him right now, or Frau Winkelvoss, they could just go on looking.

The woman went out to make coffee, proper coffee, she told him, from the West, Lampertheim, sent to her by one of her uncle's cousins who'd stayed there after the war and married a German. An engineer or something; they were doing well. She came straight back in – wearing slippers now – and took half a bar of chocolate out of the cupboard, which she broke up and put in a little bowl: Western chocolate. Then she went out again, and it became apparent that she would keep popping in and out all the time.

People were talking loudly in the kitchen. The woman seemed to be being hauled over the coals by the other tenants for bringing someone home: what was she thinking, dragging all sorts back here, and, to cap it all, a German! And then making coffee for him, expensive pure ground coffee! A door slammed, and a man yelled from the adjacent room that he had a nightshift, and if they didn't quieten down right now he'd beat them all to a pulp.

After a couple of minutes the woman came back into the room accompanied by her sick daughter. Would it be all right for her to lie down again in here? She was sick, and they didn't know what would become of her. The daughter was a young woman, and her name was Maria. Wearing a baggy dressing gown, she stood in front of the gilt-latticed glass in the wall unit and ran her fingers through her curls. Then she turned to Jonathan, who had risen to his feet. She held out her hand and asked whether he had seen the bicycle on the other side of the street. It seemed very odd to her that it was parked there. Surely it must mean something. And how had he happened to stray in here? Presumably he was making a study of how well people lived in Poland.

Later Jonathan was unable to recall what else she had said. He remembered that she had shaken his hand; he knew that hers had been limp and clammy, that she had gone on talking and had lain down again on the sofa without further ado, slipping under the blanket in her dressing gown.

He had heard on a number of occasions that there were attractive girls in Poland, but so far Jonathan hadn't spotted any ravishing beauties on the streets of Danzig: they were shot-putters rather than javelin throwers. The beautiful ones are probably in the fish factory, he thought, filleting ocean perch.

Maria was no beauty either; she wouldn't have been any good for tourism advertisements. She was full-figured, with short, sturdy legs. Her face was puffy, as if she'd been crying a lot recently.

She's a silent-film beauty, thought Jonathan. She could have been in a Buster Keaton film, riding pillion on a motorcycle, side-saddle, in a beret, her white dress fluttering behind her like a veil. Or the Persil lady, all in black, he thought. He pictured the wall of a house in Berlin, the faded Persil advertisement plastered on it from 1935: it was near the Schlesischer Bahnhof, where the Galician Jews would arrive before going on to open a junk shop in the fifth back courtyard of a tenement building.

The house was shaking from the wood-chopping in the basement. The mother came back in again and put on the table, with plates and little silver spoons, some cake left over from Sunday, and Jonathan learnt that Maria was always having strange thoughts – the bicycle, over there, on the other side of the street – that refused to go away. They became an obsession, circling round and round her head, thoughts of devils and the end of the world. As her mother talked about it, Maria lay there listening to her inner voice to see what the netherworld had to say. The outline of her body, the jutting pelvis and narrow shoulders, protruded against the blanket; she had pulled it right under her chin, bundling herself up. Her short curly hair had not been washed recently, and there were bottles of pills on the table, lying around the way they do when a suicide is discovered.

The kettle whistled, and the mother went out again. Jonathan was alone with the girl, and at leisure to examine the floor covering. It was linoleum, with a similar pattern to the one in Isestrasse in Hamburg. He told her that this linoleum covering was probably very valuable; Kolaszewski and so on. It'd be snapped up in the West; the tiles in the stairwell too, fifty marks apiece, you'd just need to find someone to remove them. Then he told her that he was a journalist and that he was preparing a car rally for motoring journalists here in Poland, which he'd never done before and actually found pretty pointless – he couldn't even drive – but it was well paid. And then he even asked – although he knew such a suggestion was absolutely ridiculous because it could never be put into practice – would she like to come along for the ride in the back of the car, an eight-cylinder Santubara? There was a spare seat; he could arrange it. It might be a distraction for her.

Although she had turned away she was listening. All of a sudden she turned back, propped herself up, looked at Jonathan and asked, 'Who's to blame?'

She lowered herself back down and said again, 'Who's to blame?'

She knew what she was talking about, and Jonathan knew, but he couldn't bear this sort of generalization; he had to counter it. You won't find one person who is to blame for everything that goes on in the world, he thought; you won't get your hands on him. And he remembered a poster he had seen in the Rocky Mountains, in a souvenir shop, an illustration of American Indians being slaughtered.

Who was to blame? He pictured the child at the airport with the pink teddy bear, and he pictured the gypsy women and the old spectacles in the drawer at Albert Schindeloe's shop; and his mother in Rosenau, on the church steps, her dress stained with blood.

The gilt-framed picture on the wall showed a young mother lying in a meadow, holding her child above her head, a ring of angels hovering round about.

Outside, through the window – he only noticed it now – you could see one of the needle-pointed steeples of the Marienkirche; and he thought of Münchhausen with his horse hanging from such a steeple, Münchhausen riding the cannonball; Hans Albers – who played him in the film – with his shining eyes, and the ball he held between his knees was the earth. Jonathan wondered whether there was a proverb he might quote at this juncture – 'Goodness is its own reward' or some such thing. There was bound to be a proverb that encapsulated all the wisdom of the West, some simple means of banishing bad thoughts.

In the meantime Frau Kuschinski had come back in with the flowered coffee pot. She poured coffee into the cups, all of which had a different pattern. The cake was excellent, probably baked with lard. Jonathan had never eaten a cake quite like it. It was accompanied by a little glass of cherry liqueur; the sugar had crystallized in the bottom of the bottle. The silver spoons had belonged to Germans; she still thought about that, said Frau Kuschinski. Exchanged for a piece of bread right after the war by frightened people living in a cellar in the ruins, chased away whenever they showed their faces.

Frau Kuschinski set about doing the laundry, taking items out of the basket, folding and sorting them, all the while holding forth about her daughter's medical history. She'd been studying German philology, in her seventh term – 'The comparative in the works of Wieland'. Always lost in thought, even as a child; then, out of nowhere, these strange, sudden moods, obsessing about a bicycle on the other side of the street that's sometimes there and sometimes not, never a sign of the owner, and about the end of the world in every form; and all the doctors uninterested and uninformed. She should go for a good long walk, they'd told her, she wasn't getting enough oxygen. And the university kept sending letters asking how long this illness was going to go on, saying that it wasn't acceptable for her to be absent for weeks on end.

'What's going to come of all this?' said the mother. 'These

stupid, stupid thoughts.' About the bicycle across the street: sometimes it was parked there and sometimes it wasn't. Or someone was listening at the door, you could actually hear their head rubbing against the wood. She'd said again and again that her daughter should stop thinking these thoughts, that this brooding was destroying what little happiness they'd managed to build here. First her husband had been run over by a lorry loaded with tree-trunks and now, as if she didn't have enough to worry about, her daughter was sick.

Who is to blame, of what misdeeds
Are we accused?

Again and again the woman urged Jonathan to drink coffee and eat. 'Eat,' she said, 'eat! Eat some more . . .' Jonathan had crossed his legs and was holding the cup politely with both hands.

Then she held up the little medicine bottle – *O come down, thou precious phial* – which had contained the elixir that had, apparently, helped. Jonathan took it from her and saw that the label was already completely worn away. This medicine would help soothe the disordered, swirling stream of thoughts in this young woman's brain provided it was taken regularly and in the correct doses. It presumably had an effect that was somehow both sedative and stimulating.

Jonathan took a sharpened pencil stub from his jacket pocket and wrote down the name of the medicine in his notebook, promising that he would get hold of some soon in Hamburg. He wondered whether he could somehow work this visit into his article. The pencil had been with him since Vienna; he'd written an article about Viennese coffee-houses with it. Under his window that day they'd been tearing up the road, its entrails on display, pipes and cables of every diameter, and he'd kept on writing amid all the hammering and crashing. The road in Maria's head was being torn up too; a hot syrupy soup was welling up inside her, forming bubbles, and she put her hands over her ears and stamped her feet to soothe her soul again.

The practical Frau Kuschinski decided it was better if Jonathan took the bottle with him in case he wrote anything down wrong, and Jonathan put it in his pocket.

A boy came in. He was Maria's little brother, and he was happy that they were having cake and chocolate.

'Who's to blame?'

He wasn't the least bit surprised that a strange man called Jonathan was sitting there. Perhaps he mistook him for a doctor, deciphering the writing on the little brown ribbed bottle with the white cork.

This is a motoring journalist, he was told, who drives around in a splendid car. Perhaps, if the boy was very, very good, he could go with them sometime? Instead of Maria, who can't, of course, because she's sick.

Jonathan confirmed what the woman had said and described what a wonderful car it was, eight cylinders, goodness knows what horsepower. Perhaps the boy could come to the hotel tomorrow, it wouldn't be a problem for him just to sit in the thing for a while. The boy talked about how someone had jostled him or chased him away and what he'd said to them. This was a bad idea, because Maria propped herself up and cross-examined him closely about whether the man been wearing a checked cap with a peak.

Jonathan listened, although he didn't understand anything, and Maria lay down again under the blanket, wrestling with her dark thoughts, and the mother stood silhouetted darkly against the window. He sensed that the magical moment had passed. He let the young woman lie on the sofa, her bones jutting against the blanket, let her mother darken the window as she shook out twisted items of laundry, and turned to the child, who – if one could say that of a boy – was beautiful, with a rare kind of beauty. The formula for beauty that no one has yet deciphered. Perhaps Maria too had been this beautiful once, back when she still went skating and didn't care whether or not people turned to look at her.

Jonathan explained to the boy what a digital display was, then he tore an empty page from his notebook, seized the scissors lying on the table and cut a car, freehand, from the paper. It more or less resembled the wondrous Santubara, and he drove it around the table going *brumm, brumm!* He had been told on a number of occasions that he was good with children.

It was great, in principle, that the boy wanted to come for a drive, said Jonathan, but of course he'd have to ask first if it was possible. Just sitting in it for a bit, though, he reckoned they could do that, no problem. And then everyone remembered that tomorrow was a school day, so it simply wouldn't be possible.

Jonathan eventually brought this childish play to an end. He said he would get hold of the medicine and send it, as agreed, once he was back in Hamburg and writing his article. It would take time, though, and would be tricky, because he had to find an unusual angle for the article, and that would require all his energy. Writing wasn't easy, after all. He stood in the living room with his head touching the too-small glass prism lamp; he shook first the boy's hand then the woman's. He would have liked to shake hands with Maria too, but she kept her hands under the blanket, completely absorbed in thoughts of heaven, earth and hell. The scissors! That was what was on her mind. The white paper had been cut to pieces by the scissors – that had to mean something, surely? One knee was sticking out from under the blanket. Jonathan saw this bare knee for just a hundredth of a second, and it was beautiful.

11

The little party had dinner in the green lounge of the Orbis Hotel. The tables were separated by trellises entwined with plastic flowers, and air conditioning blew dust across the plates. What thick crockery they have here; and what about those weird tin forks?

They served a good beer – Okocim – with a cheerful head, as Herr Strohtmeyer put it, and beetroot soup for a hundred zlotys, and smoked salmon for five hundred zlotys, with *dekoracja* that cost another thirty zlotys. You couldn't get caviar for five pfennigs here either; you'd have had to shell out two thousand three hundred zlotys per portion.

'How about that!' said Frau Winkelvoss. The meal was really quite OK. Granted, the soup was lukewarm and the salmon dry around the edges, but they could remedy that if they made enough of a fuss. The head waiter was summoned. Could these faults be remedied? And because the waiter was a little too deferential the discussion became imperious in tone.

Frau Winkelvoss was wearing a puffy blouse with twenty-six necklaces around her neck and was suffering from stage fright. She was worried about whether things would go well 'on the morrow'. They mustn't leave too late. And she was uneasy because she couldn't call home to find out how her husband and child were. How did he know the women who'd wanted his wallet were gypsies? she asked Jonathan, her tone censorious.

She'd already had one piece of bad news: Herr Schmidt had not yet arrived. This retired gastronome was supposed to inspect the gourmet restaurants that the Santubara directors were convinced lined the route of their tour and check whether they were suitable. Did they serve milk-fed lamb, or pike? During the war in France Herr Schmidt had managed a German Wehrmacht casino, and none of the reserve officers stationed there had ever had reason to complain. He hadn't been able to conjure up wild strawberries in winter, but there'd always been a little package on hand for the wives whenever the gentlemen went home on leave.

And now the man hadn't turned up.

This failure could not be laid at her door, however, so Frau Winkelvoss soon calmed down; it was merely the bad omen that troubled her. It didn't trouble her too much, though. She praised reconstructed Danzig, informing the little group in a whisper that she'd already made a good find: amid the many rings on her fingers there now sat a ring that had not sat there before. It really was awful, she said, the way the West was plundering this country.

Gdańsk! She thought it was good that the city was Polish now; it was a sort of retributive justice. She imagined there were already forces at work again in the Federal Republic of Germany that would reverse this if they could. Extraordinary to think that Günter Grass roamed this city on his scooter as a young boy in shorts.

Like Jonathan, Hansi Strohtmeyer had fallen into the

clutches of the gypsy women while sightseeing in the Old Town. His wallet had subsequently registered a one-hundred-mark shortfall. He was worrying about how he would explain it to the border guards when they left the country. This provided a good opportunity to tell him what life was like in a Polish prison; it was no picnic in there, and he would be sure to have to share a cell with drunks who would throw up over his feet.

Once again Frau Winkelvoss objected to the talk about gypsy women; as far as she was aware, there weren't any 'gypsy women' in Poland at all. He should check his wallet again properly; and anyway, why would he do something as daft as handing his wallet over to strangers?

The door opened, and a flood of German tourists poured into the restaurant, passing through it into a separate room. It was the homeland association group Jonathan had seen in the Marienkirche. The staff were already waiting for them, and they had barely sat down before the soup was brought out.

'Thank God we got here before them,' said Hansi Strohtmeyer, 'or we'd have been waiting for ever!'

Jonathan made a mental note that perhaps his five-thousand-mark article could include a word of advice about Poles being very sensitive and how, as a German, you must behave in a nice, unobtrusive way in order not to upset them. He'd already noted some tips that might be useful for the rally participants: the opening and closing times of the Marienkirche, but if it really was closed it didn't matter, he was sure it would be possible to gain out-of-hours admission for a tourist group from the Santubara Company. Jonathan envisioned the rally participants starting with the Marienkirche as a 'curtain-raiser' to inspire a sense of the homeland. This would have to be followed by a guided walking tour of the city, which could end at the monument to the Lenin Shipyard workers. He was sure he could engineer the transition for the ladies and gentlemen from Wuppertal and Bremen – a transition from the soulless, affluent society of the West to the old Hanseatic city now known as Gdańsk. The Marienkirche first – or perhaps it was better to dive straight into the country's problems, pausing reverently in front of the Monument to the Fallen Shipyard Workers? Or have them both at the end?

There'd be a line or two of dates and facts, and perhaps a few statistics. Add those to the description of Danzig's remarkable restoration efforts, and Jonathan had almost a page and a half already. It might be a good idea to look back as well: Danzig in 1939 and 1945; first the jubilation, then the hangover. That was two pages altogether, more or less, and they'd only been on the road for a day.

'Not too much history,' the PR guy from the Santubara Company had counselled him. 'Please, not too much history.'

No, he wouldn't write anything about Borislaw III and his penchant for gouging out his adversaries' eyes, but you could hardly skip over Konrad of Masovia, who invited the Germans into the country, or the whole 'Back to the Reich' business. Or the brave Polish officials who defended the Post Office, thereby saving Poland's honour. So, start with the Marienkirche after all. Or have it at the end?

There are times when I still think
Of those days by the Baltic Sea,

When in the grey gorges and chasms
Blossom fluttered on every tree.

The homeland association people at the next table had finished their meal and were listening to a talk with a slideshow: Danzig of old, how stunning this city had once been, how shabby it was now, but you had to acknowledge all the work that had gone into reconstructing it. Sitting there so comfortably around the table, they would have liked to strike up a song in praise of their native land – the one about the pastor and his cow, perhaps – but they didn't quite dare. It could easily have been misconstrued.

Once their little group had eaten its fill for the equivalent of three marks fifty all told, they made plans for 'the morrow' and decided on their route. Jonathan insisted that the Marienburg had to be next on the agenda after Danzig, otherwise they might as well stay at home. Then they went their separate ways.

'It is clean here, you can't deny that.'

Frau Winkelvoss still had a few things to settle with reception. Would it really be necessary for the rally journalists also to hand in their passports and only get them back the next day? Berlin, Paris, New York – they were all so terribly sensitive, and surely it was in the interest of the People's Republic of Poland that these journalists wrote what a jewel this country was?

Hansi Strohtmeyer swayed into the bar, where friendly ladies awaited him.

Jonathan went and sat in the lobby for a while longer. Scarcely had he taken a seat than two Eastern European-looking men came and sat beside him, brought out pearl necklaces from the pockets of their trousers and struck up an unintelligible conversation with him. Jonathan declined to join in. He conveyed to the men that someone somewhere was waiting for him, and they had to let him go. Crossing himself would not have worked this time.

He went to his room, lay down on the bed and leafed through the typewriter book for a while. It contained illustrations of some peculiar models. It was possible that a great many clever things had been written using these very models, but so, of course, had a lot of nonsense. He regretted not being able to go round to the Kuschinskis' and bring the evening to a close within the family circle – it was already a bit late for that. His retina released the image it had absorbed that afternoon, of the three people in their little apartment, the flowery wallpaper, the bedding on the sofa and, of course, the knee. It showed that the picture was still intact; it would consolidate itself into something symbolic and stand the test of time.

12

The breakfast room was decorated entirely in white. People in sportswear were drinking Sekt; there were two excessively loud Germans with gold badges on their dangling knitted ties and briefcases beside their chairs; secretive Hungarian men with a conspiratorial air and no good reason for being there; a couple of Russian officers crumbling bread between their fingers next to an interpreter in a suit and an open wing-collar shirt. They all seemed to be waiting for something. Perhaps something unusual was about to happen? It was possible. A military patrol evacuating the restaurant? All capitalists step outside! Stand against the wall, feet apart! Like the SS in Łódź looking for black marketeers and racially inferior characters: they'd be taken away in trucks, and soon afterwards – the crack of bullets.

Jonathan sat down at the only free table – it hadn't yet been cleared – and stared at the breakfast detritus on the plates. There were cups bearing traces of lipstick, and a large fresh coffee stain.

He folded his hands under his chin and thought of his girlfriend, Ulla. What a pity she hadn't come along; he could have discussed it all with her. Frau Winkelvoss, a classic people-pleaser, and Hansi Strohtmeyer – there was more to him than met the eye. More substance than style. How could he ever have mistaken him for a chauffeur?

Just at that moment the door opened and the homeland association entered in single file. The ladies had outsize jars of instant coffee under their arms to revive those who were particularly grumpy in the mornings. They were nice ladies, mums and grannies who had their feet firmly on the ground. You could tell that the men also had their feet on the ground, although one or two were looking a little wobbly.

Jonathan observed the waitresses, who were slouching about as if they'd been partying all night; they were reluctant to serve anyone but would make the effort if it became absolutely necessary. It had been a while since their last training course. The Western guest is king, they'd been told; he brings us foreign currency with which to build our socialist state. And so they made the effort, again and again. You didn't want to lose your job just because you hadn't put out fresh rolls. There were a couple of promising ones among them who approximated to the European ideal of the beautiful Polish woman, but they all showed signs of having a poor diet. Bad sausages ruin the complexion. They wouldn't stand a chance in Hamburg. Was there any one among them who could have been assigned to the Santubara crew? Probably not, unfortunately.

Then Hansi Strohtmeyer appeared, freshly shaved and smelling of Eau de Cologne. A tweed jacket with leather patches on the elbows and a shirt that was clearly tailor-made, but worn with jeans (these may have been tailor-made too, but surely not). It seemed strange somehow to see him dressed in perfectly ordinary clothes – a racing driver who had crossed the Sahara and whose face bore the marks of his accidents like duelling scars. Jonathan wasn't surprised when Hansi Strohtmeyer told him he owned a Range Rover and a Mercedes 560 SEC. And an 'Anteater' – a Golf GTI that his wife used to go and fetch the bread. So Strohtmeyer owned three cars and a yacht. There was clearly money to be made in motor racing. Which was obvious, really; why else would anyone expose themselves to such danger?

The table was filthy, Hansi said. 'Is that our bird?' he added, meaning the waitress assigned to their table. 'Come on, love, let's clean up a bit over here.' And the girl did, in fact, come immediately; she hadn't responded to Jonathan's signals.

Finally Frau Winkelvoss appeared. She'd just been on the phone to Germany, she said: Herr Schmidt wouldn't be joining them until later, which was quite a blow. You simply couldn't rely on anyone.

She praised the fact that they'd been able to take a shower in this hotel without a problem and was astonished that all the Poles were so friendly. To us Germans! After what we did to them. A third of the population exterminated and all the towns and cities destroyed!

They ate scrambled eggs, which had been made with condensed milk; it was also irritating that they only had *sweet* rolls. Frau Winkelvoss took one white pill and one red pill from a packet. She thought it was all wonderful. Condensed milk – why not? Better than nothing, she said, when you considered how little the Poles had to eat under German occupation. Now they were giving away everything they had! Then she asked Jonathan whether it really was absolutely necessary – the Marienburg, she meant. Was anyone still interested in that stuff these days? A fortress? Everyone was sick to death of militarism. Her brother-in-law was in the Bundeswehr; what an idiot! She thought they ought also to show the achievements of socialism; this was a young, up-and-coming country after all. Factories perhaps, or a shipyard? The people all looked so optimistic.

'I'm going to hit the road,' said Herr Strohtmeyer. Outside the hotel he took delivery of the car, freshly washed, lubricated and tanked with Western petrol, everything 'tippety-top' again, and he chatted a bit with Herr Schütte, who brought him up to speed on the latest racing results in Formulas 1, 2 and 3. He'd be driving on ahead to Marienburg, in case anything should happen.

The Santubaras had thought of everything. On the back seat was a basket containing sandwiches and a bottle of vodka. There was also a woollen blanket and even some change in the glove compartment for the penalty tickets which, as a foreigner, you were almost certain to get in this country.

Jonathan was the last one down. They were waiting for him.

'About time,' they said, but everyone was quite calm. As a formality, he was offered the front passenger seat, which had something to do with the assessment of his social status: he was a man of letters, after all; they'd read his story about the Provençal wine cellar. Jonathan declined. This was what he had been expected to do; they immediately capitulated and held the back door open for him. It wasn't the kind of offer you made twice.

Jonathan, who had never possessed a driving licence, settled into the back and was quite content. Here he had a little footrest, an adjustable reading lamp and an illuminated ashtray. He could spread out his papers, and he had an armrest too, which was not provided in the front seat of this ultra-modern car. It folded up, and you could install a bar underneath in case of emergency.

In the front he might have had to talk to Strohtmeyer about races across the Sahara, and Frau Winkelvoss's hot breath would have intruded on him from behind. Jonathan placed the wonderfully light woollen blanket over his knees, relishing the luxury of it. He would appropriate the blanket, he decided. It could have been meant as a gift. He was curious to find out what Strohtmeyer's driving was like. He'd expected squealing tyres, but the opposite happened: the car purred away. Oh, what a pleasure it was to ride in! You didn't feel the gear changes at all; in fact, you didn't have any sense of it being *driven* – it *drove*. How many inventions had come together to manufacture this cutting-edge product of human ingenuity: gears, ball-bearings, leverage, hydraulic transmission systems . . . not to mention petrol. And the brilliant concept of filling rubber tyres with air. Jonathan imagined the terrific speed of the pistons pounding up and down in the cylinders, hour after hour, in-exhaustible, without making a sound. A slight buzzing perhaps; really more of a hum. He had the absurd idea that he should place his forefinger on the road as a marketing gimmick; the car would roll over the finger without squashing it because he would place it exactly in the groove of the tyre's tread. . .

To distract himself he thought a bit more about the amber necklaces he'd seen in Danzig. ('Bastard!') He would have to bring something back for his girlfriend, he was aware of that. The four-colour print of *The Last Judgement* wasn't enough. Perhaps a coffee-table book about Stutthof concentration camp?

He watched the city vanish through the rear window; the Marienkirche, reappearing against the backdrop of the reconstructed harbour; a dilapidated factory; ruins with little birch trees growing on them. The abundance of impressions he had absorbed lessened with every kilometre. The gypsy clan shrank; the amber dealer blurred . . . The mental photograph he had preserved of the Kuschinskis remained on top; this would not fade so easily.

The region they were driving through could have been near Bad Zwischenahn, around the lake, with houses from Schleswig-Holstein: it exuded a cosy sort of atmosphere. It was also a bit monotonous. Unfortunately, Jonathan's view ahead was obscured by Frau Winkelvoss's headrest. He shifted his position slightly, and then it was all right.

Frau Winkelvoss was happy that this trip meant she got four days' extra holiday. 'In the sun,' she said. 'It looks as if the weather will hold until the next phase of the moon. So you think the Marienburg is worth visiting?' she asked Jonathan, turning to face him. 'Is it some sort of ruin? Like those things you see lying along the Rhine?' What was that river they'd just driven across? she demanded of Hansi Strohtmeyer. The Oder? No, it was the Wisła.

Jonathan's education had been sound, and this now stood him in good stead. He recalled that the Wisła – the Weichsel – was the only unregulated major river in Europe, and as a result it was constantly silting up because the Poles were incapable of keeping their waterways in good condition. He also knew, of course, that the Weichsel had had a tragic role to play in February 1945, and he resolved to ask his uncle how he had managed to get across what was in fact a pretty wide river. A picture arose in his mind's eye of a convoy, grey on grey, stretching into the distance, just a dark line, a sweeping curve: people streaming back into the Reich as, centuries earlier, they had poured into the east.

Jonathan popped a piece of marzipan in his mouth. With his notebook on his knees he jotted down: 'Time reference!' He also wrote that they had been overtaken by a Polish officer on a motor scooter – 'A Blendax,' according to Strohtmeyer. He was obviously a man who didn't stick to the law, as he was going pretty fast.

People like that eventually fall off those things, thought Jonathan, resolving that if that were to happen he would not permit himself to feel any pity.

A quarter of an hour later they were stopped. They'd been driving too fast, said the policeman, stepping out of the hedge like a footpad. This was a civilized country, not a place for hooligans. Strohtmeyer cracked open his supply of small change.

A dead cow in the ditch. Driving for eight kilometres behind a lopsided lorry which, when Strohtmeyer was finally able to overtake it, immediately turned right. Intensively planted gardens on both sides, but scorched fields. 'What would German nature conservationists have to say?'

Motorized wheelchairs with yellow canvas canopies; cars with spare wheels on the roof. Jonathan noted it all down, wondering what unusual angle he was supposed to find in his notes and whether he would ever be able to use them.

The two in front had quite a lot to do. They had to write the route book, which would ensure the rally participants didn't end up God knows where. Strohtmeyer dictated: 'Take the 7, direction Warszawa . . . After three kilometres an old barn with no roof tiles on the left; keep going straight on. Two kilometres. Watch out, pot-hole!' And Frau Winkelvoss wrote it all down. Hansi Strohtmeyer laughed at three-wheeled vehicles, so she lectured him: Why not? Why not drive a three-wheeler? This prompted him to remind Frau Winkelvoss that the object of their current trip was to sell eight-cylinder cars.

It was idiotic, she said, that the Polish tourism ministry had banned them from marking the route with little Santubara flags. It would have made everything much easier. Now they had to record it all in the route book instead.

'Nought point eight kilometres, row of white willows on left . . .'

At first Jonathan listened with interest: chickens cross the road the same way all over the world. Hansi Strohtmeyer was smoking aromatic foreign cigarettes, and the smell wafted back to him. He thought of his uncle, saw the heavy cart pulled by the two horses, creaking over the icy road, and on the cart the farmer's wife who had suckled him. He saw her – bare-breasted, triumphant – as Mother Earth. My mother breathed her last, he thought; but at that moment it seemed to him rather less worthy of mention. So many mothers breathed their last here back then. His uncle's resemblance to Julius Streicher, the anti-Semitic publisher. How was it possible that two people, one a criminal, the other a good and decent man, could resemble each other so closely?

And, of course, he thought of Maria – 'Who's to blame?' – and resolved to buy her medicine as soon as he got to Hamburg. He even considered calling his girlfriend, Ulla, to ask her to get hold of a prescription. How strange; he couldn't recall his own phone number.

After fifty-five kilometres they came to a road sign, MALBORK/ NOWY DWÓR, indicating that they should turn right. A break first, perhaps?

Hansi Strohtmeyer drove the car into the bushes; they got out and took some deep breaths. Jonathan stretched: it wasn't quite as comfortable in the back of the car as it had at first seemed. They sat down beside each other on the roadside embankment and inspected the food basket. It contained some Dutch biscuits that were 'unbelievably tasty', as Frau Winkelvoss put it.

On a low hill nearby was a windmill with six sails, one of which had broken off. Its door swung open and shut, and in the nearby meadow a stork was poking about, looking for frogs. Standing on one leg, it dragged them out of the moisture and swallowed them alive. In this case, being eaten equated to death by suffocation. You'd slide down the gullet – did it have grooves? – into the stomach, where injection nozzles would leap into action on all sides. The creative urge that had designed this creature had been not human but divine. Here too many different kinds of ingenuity had combined to effect such specialization. The red 'stockings', for example – why red?

It was a dirty stork, incidentally, with an unkempt grey belly. A Polish stork, Strohtmeyer joked, but Frau Winkelvoss would have none of it. She had seen a great many dirty storks in Germany as well.

Strohtmeyer crept towards the creature; perhaps the bird would allow itself to be stroked. He managed to get within fifty paces easily enough and held out his hand as if he had frogs' legs in it. But the bird looked the other way and eventually flew off.

Jonathan stared into the ditch looking for clues. If you were to dig here you'd be sure to find a leather strap, he thought, the harnesses of fallen horses that had slipped on the icy road and never got up again. Or human remains? Any skeletons dug up here wouldn't be sent to the dissecting room; they'd immediately be put back in the ground – there were more than enough of them around here. Science would not be able to draw any conclusions from these. Perhaps there were some reels of film to be unearthed, hastily buried. Reels that would enable him to watch the trail of refugees crawling through the ice storm. Wounded soldiers standing in the road, hoping for a lift. They plead with the farmers, stretch out their bloody limbs towards them, but the farmers look away.

Was it the stork that did it? As they drove on, Frau Winkelvoss started telling them the story of her child, who was adopted. Between entries in the route book she talked about how difficult it was to get hold of a child. All told, it had cost ten thousand marks – at least!

Jonathan followed their route on his German map. He read the pretty village name 'Marienau', and shortly afterwards 'Brodsack'.

Had he made a note about them seeing the stork? Frau Winkelvoss asked between entries. She turned to face him in her comfortable seat, adapted to fit the contours of the body. After all, his report needed to focus on the positive too. The fact that the stork was allowed to live here and poke about for frogs to its heart's content definitely compensated for the broken windmill. The German nature conservationists' toad tunnels had nothing to do with it.

13

All of a sudden the Marienburg appeared before them. A sign announced MALBORK. There was the river, which everyone knows is called the Nogat and is, surprisingly, still called that. Beyond it, like a picture postcard, surrounded by allotments, was the Teutonic Order's greatest fortress, the Marienburg: sacked, ruined, rebuilt, then burnt down and rebuilt again. It looked a bit mottled, but all in all it was intact and unmistakable. It had stood for seven hundred years, noble, proud, haughty. At one time the Order was praised for its strict moral code; later the knights were hated for their despotism, and then the fortress fell; the last Grand Master was forced to flee through the back door.

'Oh, it's *that* one!' said Frau Winkelvoss, who had perhaps heard about it in school during lessons about the eastern regions. Maybe they'd seen a slideshow and drawn coats of arms afterwards. She was pleased she was getting a chance to see this evidence of German history. But forty kilometres outside Danzig? That was a huge detour! Would the journalists be prepared to come? Culture was all very well, but the clients were supposed to be test-driving the cars . . .

Bridge Gate, High Castle, Grand Master's Palace, Grand

Commander's Dansker – Jonathan could identify everything perfectly. The Madonna was missing, the monumental sculpture on the external wall of the chapel whose smile had greeted the Knights of the Order from afar. The Russians had used it for target practice. Perhaps they would still find little pieces among the rubble, from which the miraculous image could be restored? Surely there were enough photographs of it?

Jonathan would have liked to have given the picture time to sink in; ideally, he would have settled down there for a while with hat and stick. He asked them to stop, got out and sat on a bench by a snack stand beside the quietly flowing waters of the Nogat. He hummed 'On the pale shores of the Saale . . .' under his breath and watched some children playing in the wreck of a car. Frau Winkelvoss stood beside him, stopwatch in hand, and Hansi Strohtmeyer didn't even get out of the vehicle; he leafed through his motoring magazines, then combed his hair. Having done that, he reached for Jonathan's pocket camera on the back seat and took a photo of the stand, the Marienburg in the background and Jonathan, dreaming, in front of it.

They drove over the bridge into the little town. They weren't here to have fun, after all. The road wound back and forth before Hansi Strohtmeyer finally drove into the castle's tourist car park. They had scarcely got out before they were surrounded by children wanting biros.

'This is like India,' said Strohtmeyer.

Jonathan reached inside his coat, which was hanging up in the car, and took out the chocolate bar he had pocketed on the aeroplane. He held it out to the children and a boy grabbed it. Jonathan was about to say, 'Don't forget to share!', but the boy had already run off, the others at his heels. And that was that. Jonathan nearly ran after them to ensure that fairness prevailed, but didn't, because he was afraid of making a fool of himself.

'No point,' said Hansi Strohtmeyer, who'd seen what had happened. 'They'll never amount to anything here.'

The technicians were already there and waiting for them. They seized control of the car: bonnet up, boot open, take a look underneath as well, fill her up from jerry cans of good Western petrol. Strohtmeyer alerted them to a slight knocking sound, and fifth gear was decidedly too loud. Then they spotted a scratch in the lacquer, all the way from front to back. Someone had walked past this technological marvel and scraped a rusty nail along its side. This person had taken revenge because you couldn't buy cars like this in Poland. Or it had been one of the children for whom Jonathan had brought the bar of chocolate.

They'd need to take lacquer with them on the rally then, and emery paper. They couldn't expect a journalist to drive a scratched car.

Meanwhile, the homeland association – the people Jonathan had first seen in Danzig – snuck up on them in an ultra-modern bus. Average age sixty-seven and a half, with three grandchildren who'd had to promise their grandfather never to forget that all this had once been German. The bus was probably also carrying a stretcher for the ninety-year-old woman.

A little to one side stood three students and their teacher from Bremen, probably a delegation from the Socialist Pupils Council of the Rosa Luxemburg Comprehensive. When they spotted the old people they fell silent. They wanted to see what sort of fascist revanchism was being played out over here and watched suspiciously to see what would unfold. They'd have to keep their distance from the wrinklies; they didn't want to get lumped in with ultra-reactionaries. Then back home they would stand up in front of the plenary session and open people's eyes to what was brewing over here. Incidentally, they had never in their lives heard of the Teutonic Order, nor did they know what the Hanseatic League had been.

You couldn't just wander in and take a look at this monument to the Germanic lust for conquest. A policeman stopped them: you had to book a tour, and it was quite a while before a woman who had command of the German language appeared. She unhooked the rope across the entrance, counted her group, and entered the number in a list of statistics. She would hand over the list that evening, and at the end of the month these numbers, combined with other numbers, would end up on the desk of the tourism general, showing whether visitor numbers were going up or hitting rock bottom. Frau Winkelvoss was keeping a list too, noting how long they needed for this stop. She glanced at Hansi Strohtmeyer: what did he make of this nonsense? But Hansi Strohtmeyer was taking it calmly; he was interested in finding out about this fortress. He'd seen the Pyramids and the Taj Mahal, he'd been up the Empire State Building and now he was doing a fortress. He'd seen something like it before, in France, and in Sudan, in the middle of the desert.

The guided tour was less annoying than anticipated. The invasion of Poland by the German Wehrmacht was not mentioned. Presumably a retired schoolteacher, the guide stuck to the subject. She pointed out original brickwork and neo-Gothic restoration and indicated transitions between old and new, saying, 'These bricks could tell more stories than I . . .'

She even knew that it had originally taken six hundred and forty million bricks to build the castle. After the war they'd used at least as many again to restore its bullet-riddled walls. At this point a man from the homeland association stepped forward and showed the ladies the difference between old and new bricks. He knew that the old bricks had been reproduced in Malmö, whereas these here were obviously local. Let's hope they hold up! The man wrote 'Malmö cloister format bricks' on a slip of paper and gave it to the woman: perhaps she would be kind enough to pass this on to head office? The three school-children from Bremen exchanged meaningful looks.

This interruption threw the tour guide a little off her stride, but she soon collected herself. In the old days women were denied entry. 'Today, as an exception, we can come in.' This appealed to her audience; people laughed comfortably, and even Anita Winkelvoss, who had already got bored and turned away, began to warm to her.

Now she was explaining the machicolation; how boiling water would have been poured down from up there when enemies approached, but there was no need to be afraid now as the portcullis had been raised, a sign that these guests were very welcome. Her humorous tone went down well with the homeland association bus people, who perhaps had been here before, as children, with their school or with the Hitler Youth. Jonathan was rather taken with this woman too; they could use her for the rally, and he needed to adopt the same tone in his article. Broadly anecdotal but finding an unusual angle. Not too extreme, though. There was every chance there would be Christian Democrats among the test drivers as well, possibly even Bavarians; they might get angry with him and write negative things about the Santubara cars.

The young people from Bremen made a note of the word 'machicolation'. A typical example of German cruelty: they could use that in the plenary session. Couldn't she show them more machicolations, they asked the woman; and why in God's name were the iron bars on the portcullis pointed at the bottom? Had Poles been laid beneath them and tortured to death? They were already looking forward to the underground dungeons and kept checking to see if they were coming up soon – chains on soot-stained walls, mouldy straw in corners.

Jonathan was intrigued by passive defence: gates, walls, the drawbridge alone. He was impressed by the consistency of the defensive techniques; they had thought of everything. He would have liked to know where the fortress got its water from when it was besieged and how many men had been catered for here. 'Impregnable' was the word that came to him. Personally, he wasn't one to curl up like a hedgehog and assume a position of all-round defence. He saw himself more as a wild gazelle – when danger approaches you run.

The woman was able to answer all of their questions. She even knew that everyone living in the fortress ate four kilos of meat per day.

The Old Prussians, the Teutonic Knights, Grand Duke Jagiełło of Lithuania, the Battle of Tannenberg, the first and second division of Poland – she trotted out historical facts like every tour guide in every country in the world. After the war, with the fortress in ruins, there had been three factions in Poland (she told them this as well): raze the whole thing, use it for building materials or rebuild. The third faction had been victorious, and that was why she had this job.

It was said of the Prussians that when they retook the fortress in the eighteenth century they immediately tore it down, brick by brick. The Bremen high-school students couldn't use that for their dissertation; it smelt of disarmament. They only perked up again when they learnt that the Prussians subsequently turned the High Castle into a barracks. And they were clearly delighted to hear that the great refectory in the Middle Castle had been used as an exercise yard. Windows bricked up? Tiles broken off? Vaults smashed? Excellent! Typically German!

The homeland association was less enthusiastic about this information, and it didn't sit well with them at all to hear it from a Polish woman. However, the gentlemen were able to point out that the Prussians had reversed it all again. You had Friedrich Gilly to thank for that – he had drawn the ruins and shown the sketches to the Prussian king, who had put a stop to this barbarism and restored the fortress at vast expense.

Frau Winkelvoss asked Jonathan if he found this interesting. What did he think of it? He did remember, didn't he, that he was supposed to write an article about it?

At this point it started to rain. The ladies and gentlemen opened the folding umbrellas they'd brought with them or simply held newspapers above their heads, and the guide suggested they go into the buildings first and tour the courtyards at the end. Thus it was that shortly afterwards they found themselves in the Chapter House – 'Where all meetings took place,' as the woman expressed it in her studied German.

When Jonathan saw the slender pillars and the delicate vaults, he thought of his northern goddesses. Why not follow up with an article about the fortresses of the north? He took out his notebook and noted down: 'Gods of the North!' That didn't really work, though – in German grammar fortresses were feminine too.

Now the guide was holding forth about the aspects of daily life everyone is interested in. She lifted a brass cover and showed them the opening from which, in winter, warm air had flowed into the room. She also showed them the holes in the wall where you could listen to what was being said inside the church. They were shown the Treasury – empty, of course – where five point eight tons of gold were hoarded in the Order's heyday: double doors, barred windows. 'It should be noted that the accounting was very precise.' The books had not been burnt; they were in Göttingen. The homeland association gave a sigh of relief, whereupon the students permitted themselves to ask when the records would be returned.

The guide didn't respond to the youngsters' questions. She seemed to find the old people more likeable somehow. Perhaps it was because the students kept whispering to each other and looking in the opposite direction. Tour guides aren't too keen on that.

In the Treasury Jonathan's attention was caught by an old bas-relief: the twelve-year-old Jesus in the Temple, and the Holy Family looking for him. Getting lost and being looked for. Those who are looked for are not lost, he thought. And he imagined what it would have been like if he'd been left behind back then, in February 1945. 'He'll die anyway . . .' He would have been raised by strangers, Poles perhaps; and perhaps he would now be trying to earn a living here as a restorer and would get cross about Germans who made disparaging remarks about Poles. Or perhaps fate would have dealt him a different hand, and he'd have had to sell sausages at a snack stand, in which case Germans would have been very welcome.

They were now entering the Summer Refectory, where there was an exhibition of charcoal drawings by a Polish artist. Concentration-camp images in the style of Käthe Kollwitz: emaciated figures clinging to the electrified fence within the zone of fire; square-jawed SS men with Alsatians doing the rounds and laughing. The homeland association slunk past these testimonies to German history, but the teacher from Bremen perked up. He walked over to the pictures, explained to his pupils what an electrified fence was and told them you could identify an Alsatian owner at fifty paces. One of the pupils held a camera to his eye and photographed the drawings. Was there a catalogue, perhaps? And might the artist be around? They'd really like to have a word with him.

The ladies and gentlemen of the homeland association were trying to move on quickly, because one of their number had been imprisoned in Dachau and still hadn't got over it. They hadn't reckoned on being confronted with this sort of thing here; hopefully he wouldn't freak out.

How long is this exhibition here for? asked Frau Winkelvoss, calculating whether the journalists would have to see it as well. Maybe it would have an adverse effect on car sales.

By now the little group had shuffled on. Everything was explained, even the length of the passageway to the loo (sixty metres). A winged devil pointed the way; winged because one did, after all, have to hurry at such moments. They were shown the latrine, the Grand Master's Dansker, a building like a little tower. There was a hole in the floorboards through which disagreeable people were thrown into the Nogat to drown. Such people were issued with a courteous invitation, entertained with four kilos of meat apiece, then thrown into the river. When you've drunk a lot you shouldn't go swimming, that's what they used to say.

'But I suggest you do not believe this; it is only story without proof...'

Jonathan looked down through a hatch into the church. It was still in ruins. In 1945 German soldiers had holed up here to defend themselves along with their ammunition, and the whole lot had blown up.

The ladies and gentlemen of the homeland association, who occasionally gave each other meaningful looks or suppressed a laugh because certain details seemed pretty far-fetched to them, knew that after it was reconstructed the castle had burnt down again in 1959. They rubbed the woman's nose in that. Polish television had wanted to preserve the restorers' achievements on film, and in doing so something had short-circuited and it had all gone up in flames. That was true, wasn't it? Destroyed more completely than at the end of the war. So the skill of Polish electricians left something to be desired? (This was intended as a teasing remark.) The Polish guide couldn't help but confirm this; however, she got her revenge with the little cage in the courtyard where the Teutonic Knights had planned to imprison the Lithuanian general Vytautas in 1410. The Knights had thought that Lithuania would lose the battle and they would receive a great deal of money for the release of the Grand Duke, but then things had gone against them. This delighted the Rosa Luxemburg group from Bremen; they were tremendously pleased that the Germans had shot themselves so comprehensively in the foot. They also went up to the guide and apologized for the impertinence of the old revanchist bastards here, belittling Polish workmanship. Not all Germans thought this way. They wanted her to please be aware that there was another Germany too, progressively minded and on the side of peace-loving countries.

Their visit also took in the Great Refectory and the kitchen, where whole oxen were roasted on spits, coated in clay to retain the fat. Afterwards, they were keen to have a little cup of coffee. Frau Winkelvoss, who had walked the entire tour with a pink clipboard in her hand, marking a slip of paper with plus and minus signs, gave the guide a ten-mark note and alerted her to the rally, during which there were sure to be a few more ten-mark notes like this one. She wrote down the woman's name so that she and only she would have the pleasure of conducting the forthcoming tour.

The homeland association ladies handed the woman an envelope full of cash. Would she perhaps be so kind as to pass this on to the fortress administration? It had been such a pleasure to revisit this place from their childhood.

The castle cafe was reserved for the homeland association, a fact attentively noted by the students from Bremen. They sat down on the wall with cans of Coca-Cola and were pestered to death by the Polish children, who wanted to drink Coca-Cola as well. Didn't they realize that Coca-Cola was a symbol of American imperialism? said the Bremen students, miming their disdain.

In Café Zamkowa there was a little table free, and the three Santubaras were served coffee *naturalna*, a mixture of infused coffee grounds and roasted barley. Frau Winkelvoss was disappointed: she had such a craving for coffee. But they would make do; after all, there were worse things in the world. Presumably during the war there wouldn't have been any coffee here under the Germans either.

Hansi Strohtmeyer commented that the loos in the basement were in immaculate condition. You had to give them that.

14

They drove through the run-down streets of the little town of Marienburg and were promptly stopped by a police patrol. The police wanted to know whether the car was actually licensed, and hadn't they noticed they'd been driving too fast?

They prowled around the car to see if could find anything else to penalize. They peered through the windows to see who else was sitting there, and Jonathan, innocently studying his German-language map – Christburg, Preussisch Holland, such beautiful place names! – had to show his passport. Trembling, he extracted it from his jacket.

Hansi Strohtmeyer was forced to decimate the Santubara Company's stock of change, which he did fairly calmly. The policemen didn't understand the word 'receipt'. They did, however, understand that he'd told them to move along, which prompted further negotiations in broken German.

Having survived this, they drove around the corner and stopped outside a butcher's shop. Hansi wanted to order Krakauer sausages, *kiełbasa Krakowska*, which were sure to cost only a few pfennigs over here. But this shop didn't have any Krakauers, even though it had CHOICE SAUSAGES clearly written in German above the door; neither money nor fine words would buy you Krakauer sausages here. The housewives queuing for tripe looked disconcerted, as if Hansi had asked for something indecent. He could have bought some tripe, or pig's trotters, sawn off, washed and scrubbed clean with a nailbrush. The police car came sneaking along outside. What was going on now? Stopping outside a butcher's? Were they planning on parking here all day? They had to make a bit more of an effort to respect the law of the land.

Hansi Strohtmeyer conspicuously noted down the police car's number plate and said, 'Tourist office', after which they left them alone.

When he thought how friendly he had been to Poles all his life, he said, whenever he'd met them in Germany – always shown them the way and so on – they could kiss his backside! If a Pole ever asked him again how to get to the Reeperbahn in Hamburg he'd send him to the Botanical Gardens.

They drove on, towards Dzierzgoń, alias Christburg – 'Careful: downhill, then the turning's on the left!' – and, as they drove along a splendid avenue of oaks, Frau Winkelvoss regaled them with the second half of her adoption story: the prelude, how it had actually come about that they had decided to adopt another person's child. The manner of her report was different from the kind of thing she usually came out with. In dramaturgically structured speech she listed all the various things she had done to try to get her body to cooperate: meditation, diet, gymnastic exercises. Nothing had helped.

'You saved a load by not paying for the pill for years, then,' said Hansi Strohtmeyer roughly.

The depressing aspects of a gynaecological examination were emphasized with rhetorical brilliance. The fact that, as a woman, one was completely at the gynaecologist's mercy and that science still hadn't come up with alternative ways of conducting this examination was a scandal. Frau Winkelvoss proceeded to demonstrate, in the very luxurious but rather confined space of the car, how you had to sit on that most uncomfortable of chairs.

Jonathan was familiar with this. He had been to see a proctologist once; the treatment had done him good.

The car purred softly over the pot-holed road. Jonathan was fascinated by the ceramic insulators on the telegraph poles. You saw things like that in old photos of the homeland. These must be from the German period, he thought. The trees along the avenue too. They ought to chop down one of these trees and count the growth rings. A hundred years old? Did roadside trees live to be a hundred years old? Before the war, holiday bulletins from the Curonian Spit had chirped along these telephone wires: the weather's glorious, and Elke went swimming for the first time. Thomas Mann outside his house in Nidden, wearing white shoes . . . Then military dispatches were sent down the lines, triumphant at first, then depressing. Tentative enquiries from the Ruhr: mightn't it be possible to find some sort of barn in Gumbinnen where they could take shelter? Gumbinnen – that was pretty safe, surely? Then, at the end, the very last communications, as if via shortwave radio, barely intelligible: for the love of God, the Russians are coming . . .

A signalman's house, half burnt down, surrounded by lime trees from the days of empire; beeches, an overgrown garden with a broken fence, dahlias and chrysanthemums. The kind of house where bloody vengeance was exacted in 1945, first by one side then by the other. The victims' screams still caught in the treetops.

Jonathan thought he would like to live in a house like this, in complete seclusion, with a dog and no wife. Or perhaps not: at night they'd break in, knives in hand, and where were you supposed to get your bread rolls of a morning in this god-forsaken neck of the woods?

It was a comfortable drive. Unfortunately, the two up front were smoking: Egyptian cigarettes for Hansi Strohtmeyer, and matchstick-thin gold-tipped cigarillos for Frau Winkelvoss. Clouds billowed into the back with every puff and were not dispersed by the ingenious internal ventilation system, which, like car-ventilation systems all over the world, proved useless. The stream of air blasting out of the nozzles blew Jonathan's thin hair into his face. Eventually he opened the window and left it open, even though Anita felt a draught down her neck.

When Frau Winkelvoss had completed the second chapter of her narrative – the idea of adopting a child, of saving it, and the discovery that there was a waiting list for such an undertaking – she grew restless. She needed to go, she said, and Hansi Strohtmeyer was ungallant enough to ask whether she needed to do a number one or a number two.

She needed to spend a penny – to decant the coffee, to be precise; she couldn't help it.

It certainly was a peculiar sight: this woman, in her puffy blouse, wound about with scarves of every colour of the rainbow, laden with twenty-six necklaces (and a brass-studded belt about her waist), teetering off into the woods in black harem trousers and high-heeled shoes. Had there been monkeys in these woods they would have followed her, swinging from branch to branch.

The men also got out to stretch. Then they strolled in the opposite direction, along a narrow, asphalted road blocked by a rusted gate that hung crooked on its hinges. A sign on it in Polish said there was no thoroughfare, so they climbed over it to explore. No one had driven down the road in a long time; all sorts of plants had pushed through the asphalt and broken it up.

'This is incredible,' said Hansi Strohtmeyer. 'They could make loads of films here!' The Russian one – that film, what was it called? It reminded him of that.

Eventually they came across a half-ruined factory, the kind you saw in Germany if you travelled by train and looked attentively out of the window. Only the outer walls of the main halls were still standing, and the chimney had collapsed. It was almost completely silent; the only sound was the rustling of trees, with the blue sky and two birds of prey circling high in the air.

Jonathan remembered the 'Documentation of the Expulsion' he had bought in Hamburg. There was one report about an abandoned factory that had served as an 'internment camp' for Germans, a camp where people had starved, or been beaten to death, or had perished of typhus. Horrible details, officially preserved for ever and a day. Had it been this factory?

Hansi Strohtmeyer smashed the last few windows. He told Jonathan he was an angler and chatted about all the fish he had caught.

Jonathan wondered why he didn't just leave the fish alone. If you wanted to eat something you could always open a tin.

*

They turned back. What big trees these were; a hundred years old at the very least. And the Poles were bound not to have the first idea about forest management. Hadn't they shot the last of the wild horses? And the European bison? Think what you could do with all this by applying free-market methods. Breed deer and let West German capitalists shoot them for a fee.

In a clearing they stumbled on a graveyard overgrown with ivy. It turned out that Polish forced labourers were buried here, and there were two Soviet graves beside them, little pyramids with red stars on top.

'Wonder where they dumped the Germans!'

Frau Winkelvoss, meanwhile, was not having an easy time of it. Returning from doing her business, she saw two men standing beside the car, messing about with it like baboons in an automobile zoo. One climbed into the freshly washed vehicle and sat twiddling the steering wheel; the other had put on Hansi Strohtmeyer's Prinz Heinrich cap and started rummaging in the picnic basket. Anita couldn't hide any longer: they'd already seen her; she couldn't run away.

So she had to endure the two men hitting on her. The one who had just taken a swig from the vodka bottle corked it back up and started counting the chains around her neck. Their virile overtures were already pretty far advanced by the time Jonathan and Hansi Strohtmeyer stepped out of the woods – not a moment too soon.

For a fleeting second Jonathan considered running away. Should he stay and let himself be beaten to death? His job was to write an article about the cultural riches of the People's Republic of Poland. No one had said anything about murder, which was what now seemed to be in store for him. He could see the report in the newspaper: German journalist and famous racing driver found dead; woman repeatedly raped.

What happened next, though, wasn't murder and mayhem. The man behind the wheel revved the engine, his friend leapt in the back, and the three colleagues were left behind staring after their beautiful V8.

'Nowt to be done about it,' said Hansi Strohtmeyer, once the dust had settled. 'We'd best get cracking.'

And so off they plodded, like a gaggle of tramps. Would you believe it! Car gone, all their luggage, their passports, money!

At least Jonathan had his briefcase with him and the big map of Poland with the German place names, as well as his pocket camera. But all his notes were lost! How was he to write the article without notes, let alone find an unusual angle?

Strohtmeyer, on the other hand, had lost his peaked cap, which he'd had with him on the Africa trip, and the tweed jacket, which didn't look like much but he'd bought it in London and it had been quite expensive. Anita Winkelvoss, on the other hand, with her mountains of clothes, didn't complain – on the contrary. How nice, she said; now at last she could go on another huge shopping spree in Frankfurt.

They spent the first two kilometres itemizing everything they'd lost. Like in the war, after an air raid. It occurred to Jonathan that the Kuschinskis' address was lost as well. What on earth would they think of him when they never heard from him again?

Then Frau Winkelvoss turned her ankle. The heel of her left shoe snapped off, at which point she removed the 'worn-out old things', as she called them, flung them into the woods and walked on barefoot on her firm little feet, through the beautiful natural surroundings, with birds of prey circling above them, and all the while she longed to shout *Whoopee!* 'Isn't it great, this adventure we're having!'

Was she a child of nature, then? She circled her arms, inhaling the fresh air, and rhapsodized about rambler roses and riding. They'd bought Cariossa a pony so she could ride with the grown-ups one day. It turned out that Frau Winkelvoss's husband was the German number one in eight-horse carriage driving. After a while she grew so high-spirited that she gave Hansi Strohtmeyer a shove, and he humoured her by reeling across the road. It was a splendid road, but, alas, there wasn't a single vehicle tearing along it: no Poles, no tourists, no shiny clean West German coaches, and no motorized three-wheelers with orange canopies either.

Over the next few kilometres their hike turned into a treasure hunt. They had to gather up their belongings, which the Poles had thrown out of the car window. The first thing they found was Anita's pink clipboard, then Hansi's tweed jacket hanging in the bushes (from London, all six hundred pounds' worth) – with his passport in the inside pocket, moreover, which prompted Strohtmeyer to ask whether perhaps they had been White Poles, anti-communists. As in, people who could still muster a degree of sympathy for their fellow humans.

When at last they came to a lake, with some benches to rest on and a little car park, they saw that the Poles had behaved like Europeans, in that they had rifled the suitcases but had at least left them behind. Jonathan's bag was there too. His notes were fluttering all over the road like flurries of snow. The money was gone, of course, that was obvious, and Anita's little bracelet from Rio was missing, which made her momentarily sad. She'd picked it up so cheaply back then, when they'd gone to fetch Cariossa; but never mind, the main thing was that they were all safe and sound. As they were gathering and sorting out their things, the West German homeland association bus materialized in the distance. All three ran out into the road and waved – Stop! SOS! But the bus driver did nothing of the sort. He drove smoothly past, and the passengers looked down on them from above and wondered who these strange people were, running about in the road and waving.

Hansi Strohtmeyer took it upon himself to walk on alone and get his hands on a set of wheels. This would take some time, even though he was a racing driver. The two of them should just sit here and wait for him, he said. A massive old oak tree blasted by lightning would serve as a marker for him to find them again.

So Strohtmeyer disappeared, and the two of them grabbed their suitcases and bags and sat down on a bench and gazed out over the lake, which had once been a German lake with German fish in it, and in winter a stake had been driven into the ice for the children to skate around like a merry-go-round, and the ice was so clear you could see the fish motionless beneath it.

Anita was still disgusted by the two Poles. She couldn't just shrug it off, she said. She explained in great detail how the guy had felt her up and that the first thing she would do when they got back to Germany was have everything cleaned, obviously. She squatted down by the water and rinsed her hands and said, Ugh! It disgusted her. And Jonathan thought about the women of 1945, and what they'd endured when the Russians came.

God, that lovely car! The Poles would probably use it to transport geese!

Jonathan said he didn't think so. If a grey V8 showed up anywhere around here they'd collar the thieves in no time. No, no geese. They were bound to sell the car on the black market, to someone in Warsaw perhaps.

This thievery was also a kind of reparation.

'Just look at the nature here,' Frau Winkelvoss said finally, 'one lake after another and not a soul in sight!' What amazing resources they had; the region would be great for surfing or sailing, or simply swimming. 'Build a hotel, with a cafe – it'd be a goldmine!' There were no lakes like this anywhere any more. She was tempted to tear off her clothes and plunge into the water.

Jonathan asked if she could give a two-fingered whistle. No, Frau Winkelvoss couldn't do that; she could just do a bit of ordinary whistling and then only if no one made her laugh. Jonathan couldn't whistle either. He clapped his hands and there was an echo; but it was better if they didn't clap, otherwise some other guys might turn up and they'd be completely at their mercy.

Was it the cool breeze coming off the lake; was it his cosmopolitan attitude? Frau Winkelvoss was seeking support. She had moved in a little too close for comfort. Jonathan, however, felt no excitement. Was she trying it on? Actually, in his spotted bow-tie and Italian jacket he felt rather out of place in the great outdoors.

There was a shed nearby; it was dark and smelt of carbolineum. The high-spirited Frau Winkelvoss inspected the shed and found two boats inside. She called Jonathan over. He should come and look at this shed, there were boats in here, he should come and lend a hand.

With considerable effort they pulled one out and pushed it into the water. 'Let's sink it,' said Frau Winkelvoss. As they discovered, this wasn't all that easy.

When at last it was accomplished, Anita started babbling, not making a great deal of sense. Was he always such a killjoy? It wasn't easy for a woman to persuade a man.

Jonathan acted as if he didn't understand, and perhaps he really didn't.

Then Anita went on about what a loser her husband was – he had girlfriends all over the place; why shouldn't she, as a woman, pick up a man from time to time? This was what she didn't understand. At that moment Jonathan didn't feel like a man, more like a schoolboy with a satchel on his back and the blackboard duster sticking out of it. He didn't respond to her overtures, and eventually Anita gave up. She took off her clothes and walked into the dark, cold forest lake with outstretched arms, step by step. She stroked the surface with her hands, then finally pushed off and swam out, or in, or whatever.

15

Three hours later Hansi Strohtmeyer drove up in a rented car. He'd made lots of calls from the police station. The V8 had gone, of course, but they could count on the technicians' car in Sensburg, and everything they'd lost would be replaced. The Santubara Company, which even maintained a small symphony orchestra, would be generous in this regard. How marvellous that the car had the long scratch down the side – that would reduce its value for the thieves.

As soon as she saw Hansi Strohtmeyer, Frau Winkelvoss turned into a bit of a nervous wreck. She'd tied back her hair in a wet ponytail. She wanted to take the quickest route to the hotel and urged Hansi Strohtmeyer to drive down the tree-lined avenues as fast as possible; they knew what these looked like by now, they were basically all the same. The German Automobile Association should visit; it would get all of those trees cut down!

They passed through several villages and towns, which Jonathan ought to have stopped to look at. He was tracing their journey on the map and in the travel guide and hoped he would quickly pick up on any culture here, things he should suggest for the rally.

They raced through the villages, in every one a shuttered kiosk selling fruit – *frukty* – washing on the fences, goats, sheep, houses with tin roofs. A cow standing by the side of the road raised its head. 'Don't forget there's a sump under the engine,' said Frau Winkelvoss as they thundered over the cobblestones. They had a Polish licence plate now, so no one stopped them any more.

Stooks of corn in the fields; a horse being beaten because it couldn't pull a cart; a calf, trussed up in a wooden cage on a tractor trailer with rubber tyres; giant umbellate flowers; a nun with a wheelbarrow; half-constructed buildings, started and abandoned – all slid past. The city of Allenstein – oh God, yes: now Olsztyn. 'Write it down for all time.' The Germans had abandoned this town in a hurry in 1945: a trip to the cinema one evening; next morning the Russians were there. The whole town fell into the hands of the glorious Soviet army undamaged, and then they'd torched it, even the warehouses, although they could have made good use of the stuff that was in them.

Factories of all kinds, rubbish dumps, big groups of people by every bus. They did stop in Allenstein after all.

The first thing they saw was a drunk lying across the pavement. People were walking around him. You got that in Canada too, said Hansi; drunken Indians – he'd seen them in Calgary once, rows of them, all huddled together. But a girl with a cow on a bomb site right in the centre of town – that was a new one on him.

While Hansi Strohtmeyer went to make a phone call to see whether the technicians' car would be available tomorrow – these people are never there when you need them – Jonathan wandered all over the town making notes. The castle with the Copernicus museum (closed on Mondays), a city gate, and the Jakobskirche, on a par with his northern goddesses. In the market, farmers and traders had spread out their wares on the pavement: cabbages, carrots, home-made sweets, Western clothes, rusty taps and second-hand shoes. It was like a Hamburg flea market.

Jonathan was about to head back to the car when he noticed an old man with a stain on his trousers like the patch on a pair of riding breeches. A few books lay in front of him: Russian classics, a song book, newspapers – and a photo album. Jonathan picked it up and leafed through. It documented the life of a German family, beginning in 1922 with a picture of the bridal couple. The last photos were from 1944, with a picture of the father who had fallen in battle. The year 1936 also featured: the Berlin Olympics, two fat women with tiny handbags in front of the Brandenburg Gate. Every swastika had been carefully scribbled out.

Frau Winkelvoss stayed in the car with the windows up. Teenage boys were lurking around the vehicle. She felt as if she'd been left here to stew in her own juice; she'd been waiting forty-five whole minutes, she said to Jonathan when he asked her how she'd got on.

Soon Hansi was back as well. 'All right?' he said. He was thinking about all the dogs in this town; there were lots of them, all mongrels. If you were to try to separate them again, all those different breeds, you'd really have your work cut out. He'd found a restaurant; perhaps they could eat something there?

They counted the money Jonathan had saved, then the two

men walked with Anita, one on either side, and took a seat in the cafe, which looked as if it dated from the 1930s. They tried to convey to the waitress that they were hungry – 'Make din-dins!', as Hansi put it. 'Eat . . . *essen* . . . *manger* . . . !' Apparently this restaurant, where a slice of buttercream-filled cake once cost thirty-five pfennigs, only served beer. Just then, however, the landlord came over and offered them fish salad.

While they were waiting for the salad, which the landlord went to buy from the shop next door, Jonathan looked in his travel guide. In 1920, 97.7 per cent of the people of Allenstein voted for Germany and only 2.3 per cent for Poland. He wondered whether Germans still accounted for even 2 per cent of the population of Allenstein.

The restaurant still looked pretty damn German, though. Equalization of burdens: Jonathan wondered how much the former proprietor had received in compensation.

He took his camera out of his pocket and snapped a couple of pictures of the wall, which was adorned with art-deco-style panelling. It would have been better if he hadn't, though, because a few seconds later some men in the background got up and approached him menacingly. What did he think he was doing taking photos of them? and so on.

Jonathan tried to explain what a wonderful construction this wall was, with its delicate panelling; he hadn't been photo-graphing them at all, just this wonderful structure. He tried but failed to do what Hansi Strohtmeyer had attempted with the men in the woods and bring some objectivity to their disagreement. Instead, he was grabbed by the lapels, shoved against the table, and the man who'd grabbed him drew back his arm and punched him on the shoulder. He'd actually intended to hit Jonathan's chin, but it's not that easy to hit a chin; boxers don't always manage it in the ring either. There was quite a tussle, but Hansi Strohtmeyer pulled them apart, and, as they discovered, he had pretty strong arms.

When the landlord arrived with the fish salad the thugs backed off, and Jonathan and his companions took to their heels.

Layabouts, most likely, said Strohtmeyer, whiling away their time in here instead of hod-carrying on a building site. They probably thought he was going to photograph them and then maybe report them to the police.

They drove the old banger as fast as it would go, as if they were being pursued. Frau Winkelvoss handed out the last of her cough sweets to stave off their hunger.

'Good thing we didn't eat the fish salad,' said Hansi Strohtmeyer. He'd eaten fish salad in Recife once and spent three weeks in hospital.

It was quite late now; horse-drawn carts with no lights loomed up out of the darkness. The question was, would they still be able to get anything to eat in Sensburg? The technicians' car was parked outside the hotel. Hansi Strohtmeyer drove up alongside and pulled on the handbrake. Made it!

The mechanics came running up, as if wanting to make amends to Frau Winkelvoss. Naturally, they were feeling guilty. Instead of driving along behind Hansi Strohtmeyer and keeping an eye on things they'd been playing a game of skat in Sensburg. A lively discussion ensued. They'd already emptied the repair vehicle, given it another thorough clean; there was hardly any difference between this car and the one that had gone missing except that Jonathan didn't have a reading lamp in the back. Herr Schütte said he could use his torch and pressed an inspection lamp into his hand. Many a car must have been repaired in the light of its beam. It was obvious to the two mechanics that they would have to make the return journey in the old banger, and they immediately set about inspecting the thing.

The tourism general had already called, having been alerted by headquarters. He'd said how sorry he was and that when the thieves were caught they would be severely punished.

In the foyer the German homeland association tourists were swaying along to music. 'Cornflower blue . . .' As Strohtmeyer remarked, these were people who would normally book a package holiday to Istanbul, three days for ninety-eight marks.

God preserve us from wind and rain
And Germans going abroad again.

These people had no clue about the sort of experiences you could have in Poland; they'd driven here in their fully air-conditioned bus with its composting toilet and reclining seats, and would drive home in that bus as well. And now they were swaying along to their drinking songs, demonstrating a particularly German kind of merriment to the Polish staff.

The Orbis Hotel wasn't able to provide German newspapers, but it did have a bottle of vodka. This promised to be an entertaining evening!

It was late when the three of them reconvened. They could still order something to eat; the place had a decent menu. First they had bread soup with sausage, followed by duck breast. Frau Winkelvoss said the dry wine was too sweet for her, and Hansi Strohtmeyer remarked that there should be croutons floating on the bread soup; that was the way his mother-in-law had always made it. The duck breast was accompanied by oily sautéed potatoes seasoned with thyme, which elicited applause. The salad one could forget; it had been sitting on the sideboard for hours. A motorway-service-station salad was what it was.

There had been a letter waiting for Frau Winkelvoss. Herr Schmidt, the gourmet who had procured champignons for German officers in France, would be joining them in Danzig. In the meantime they could start by asking around and finding out if there was somewhere in Sensburg that served milk-fed lamb. They should just take a copy of the menu and bring it with them. She described her fear, back there in the woods, that those two filthy men would rape her, but already her tone was becoming more neutral; the story would eventually enter into part of her repertoire. Back in Frankfurt, she said, she would finally take that self-defence course she'd been planning to sign up to for ages. Kick the bastards in the balls, she could manage that.

Hansi Strohtmeyer, who had by now drunk several glasses of schnapps, dared to make an offensive remark. Rape? She was barren, wasn't she? So why was she getting so worked up? He also revealed to them that he had a thing for coaches: three hundred and fifty horsepower, just imagine! What a feeling it must be to manoeuvre a twelve-metre-long vehicle like that through narrow streets, floating softly, elegantly over the asphalt. You didn't hear the engine because it was at the back, and you didn't notice the gear changes either. And the power-assisted steering had an incredibly high ratio. He showed them how you sit when you're driving: elevated, with the window beneath you. The driver's seat could be artificially reinforced, and, of course, it was air-cushioned too. The side mirrors were enormous and electronically adjustable.

After dinner. The hotel was beside a lake, and the night was mild. In the darkness you could see that the hotel had been intended to be twice as big. The left wing, an abandoned investment, 'sat there looking rather sinister', as Hansi put it. 'Looks like they didn't have enough cash.'

They sat down at a table, and soon the waiter was bringing them one *piwo* after another, and they had the vodka they'd brought with them under the table too.

From indoors came the sound of a Polish folk-dance troupe rehearsing for a folklore festival. At the same time the German tourists were drawing attention to themselves with increasingly provocative songs, the lyrics of which the Poles, thank goodness, didn't understand.

Hansi continued to talk about his thing for coaches, and Anita Winkelvoss told them about a friend of hers who didn't have a clue about cars; she'd bought a second-hand 2CV, twelve-and-a-half horsepower, driven it around Italy and Spain and never realized it had a fourth gear.

Hansi could imitate the noise of a Trabi rolling over by cracking his knuckles. He talked about his Africa rally too, all the way across the Sahara and back, and how he'd got stranded in a river in South America. Anita Winkelvoss went on at length about how idiotic it had been of Jonathan to mistake Hansi for a chauffeur. Was he aware of how famous Strohtmeyer was in professional circles?

This romantic evening, in which the moon played its part, ended with them all completely plastered, and a long joke about a publican looking for the guest who had shat in his fan.

16

The next morning they switched to the technicians' car. Herr Schütte from the Santubara Company had sent a message: they needed to be a bit more careful now and keep an eye out for any trouble. They couldn't be constantly supplying them with new cars, after all.

There were some nice little gifts on the back seat: a grey leather writing case for Jonathan and a toiletries bag for each of them containing soap, cream and toothpaste. They also received two hundred marks apiece, which Anita Winkelvoss noted down on her pink clipboard.

Unfortunately there was no new woollen blanket. Jonathan had been looking forward to appropriating that.

There was a brief stop in town when they were pulled over yet again. A grey Santubara V8 was missing, the two policemen said. Everybody out! Could they prove that this car belonged to them?

Yes, they could prove it. But they'd been driving too fast again and were slapped with another fine.

The policemen were rather shady. Hansi had to open the boot and then the suitcases, all of which took a long time and was very suspicious. When one of the policemen started poking about in Jonathan's jacket, Hansi asked, 'Are you allowed to do that?' and that was the end of it.

Jonathan gazed out of the window. A tractor drove past with a dog balancing on the rear axle. In the villages, farmers' wives turned to look at the car; there were waving children and an avenue of white willows beside a little stream.

Whenever possible Hansi Strohtmeyer drove down the middle of the road. If a deer jumped out, he'd have a quarter of a second longer to react, he said. At one point he stopped, busied himself with something outside and got in again a few minutes later.

'What was the matter?'

'We had a flat tyre.'

Jonathan was glad they were on the home stretch. Today they would drive in a big arc, finishing in Danzig in the evening. He put the papers he'd gathered up off the road in the correct order and augmented them with a few notes from the travel guide; there was no chance of stopping now if a church hove into view.

'This looks like northern Germany.'

'Don't let a Pole hear you say that.'

It was wonderful that this car didn't have a radio either.

Undaunted, the two in the front resumed the meticulous preparation of the route book – careful: pot-holed bridge! – while Frau Winkelvoss continued her adoption story. The woman from the welfare office had kept turning up at their house: income, health, certificate of political good conduct, ancestry right back to their great-grandfathers. All of which they'd had to get translated and sent over, two ring binders full.

Oh, yes – and proof that they couldn't have children themselves.

At this point they were driving through a very pretty village that was clearly extremely old. They passed striking half-timbered houses with the arcaded porches typical of the region and a red-brick church with a high tower.

Then Jonathan cried, 'Stop!' The other two jumped – what now? – and they stopped in front of one of the old houses, which must have been protected by some sort of preservation order. Jonathan photographed it from both front and back; he also photographed the fence, which was made out of old bedframes. It would be great, he thought, if there were a village wedding coming up and they could persuade the locals to let the rally journalists take part – for a fee, of course.

Hansi Strohtmeyer went into the village shop to ask about Krakauer sausages, and Frau Winkelvoss stayed in the car to change her trousers; they were a bit too warm for the day. An old man turned up at the fence and said yes, Jonathan was right, it really was a very lovely house and in excellent condition inside as well. Would he like to take a look?

The bedframe gate was opened and Jonathan was invited in. It was indeed a lovely house, timbered, with carved pillars in front; and the barn, which must have been about two hundred years old, was worth a look as well. The Russian invasion of 1914, the Second World War, Russians, Poles, Germans – this barn had survived them all.

A young woman joined them, and they went into the kitchen. Jonathan was offered a stool; a glass of milk was put in front of him, and a horse bucket of shrivelled but extremely tasty apples, with respectable wormholes, freshly picked. These are German winter apples, thought Jonathan. He wondered whether he ought perhaps to cut a few scions from the tree and take them home to bring some variety to the apples found in West German supermarkets – *all* green or *all* red or *all* yellow. He could give the scions to the agriculture minister, who would arrange their distribution, and suddenly everyone would understand just how wonderful an apple can taste.

The milk Jonathan had been given was not all that pure; it tasted good, but there was sediment in the bottom of the glass, and Jonathan didn't drink it all.

Should he have said to the old man that the Germans had only themselves to blame for being expelled? All the university lecturers sent to concentration camps, schools closed – Poles didn't need to learn to read; forced labour, starvation. And then the business with the Jews. Should he have debated with him about the Oder–Neisse Line, argued that Stettin wasn't included?

The old man was speaking a flood of mostly incomprehensible words, in a quiet sing-song, almost to himself. The hair on the back of his neck hung over the collar of his jacket, and he still had a couple of teeth left in his head. He told Jonathan that in his youth he had served in the Polish army, then deserted, then served in the German one. Then he'd been a partisan and in the Polish army again; then he'd resettled and come here. Jonathan could understand all this because the old man occasionally mixed in German words among the Polish. He ascertained that the man had something against the Jews. Did he even rub his hands when he spoke of how the Jews were 'gone'?

Children also appeared, proper children, like the apples in the bucket, barefoot or in rubber boots and brightly coloured pinafores. One was wearing glasses, the left arm of which was missing. A dog came in as well, a proper village dog with a lot of Spitz in him; he came straight over and lay down under Jonathan's stool, which was presumably his safe spot. The children stood in the doorway and stared at Jonathan, and he felt like a figure in the Fritz von Uhde painting *The Mealtime Prayer*.

In the meantime Frau Winkelvoss had put on her black harem trousers and came teetering across the farmyard in gold-trimmed shoes with the pink clipboard balanced on her hip. Had he seen the bedframe fence? she asked Jonathan. 'Absolutely bonkers!' She happily accepted an apple from these people, who assumed that Frau Winkelvoss was Jonathan's wife. An apple, yes, but no milk, said Frau Winkelvoss, who had spotted the sediment in Jonathan's glass: cow's milk gave her allergies, little pimples – a rash. No, she'd better not have any milk.

Neighbours started appearing. They'd seen the glittering car standing outside and thought: German relatives have shown up; maybe we can tap them somehow. One of them called the Germans over; he wanted to show them something. He led them through the rhubarb patch, over a trampled fence and into the big barn, which was built on glacial boulders. The Poles immediately knew what this was about. A cupboard was pushed aside to reveal a cavity, which had clearly been used to store vast quantities of provisions: lard in milk churns, flour, a sack of sugar . . . The Germans had installed it just before the Russians invaded. The space had only been discovered the previous year.

Jonathan wanted to know whether there had been coins in there perhaps, or an old Bible. And what had happened to the people? Had anyone ever got in touch? No one understood these questions. He heard the word *militsiya* – police – but Bible? No. There was a *Biblia* over in the kitchen.

What had the village been called in German times? Jonathan asked. And the answer came: Rosenau.

Although he had studied the map very carefully – first in Hamburg, then every night in the hotel – and really ought to have known that they would pass through the village today, it was as if the desire to see his birthplace had been blotted out. Instinct had prompted him to ask Hansi Strohtmeyer to stop here of all places.

As they walked out of the barn and back to the house through a gaggle of geese, he explained to the villagers that he had been born here, on a refugee wagon; and Hansi Strohtmeyer, who had arrived in the interim, got to hear that his mother had breathed her last giving birth to him.

The old man immediately understood what Jonathan was telling them and passed the information on. This gentleman was born here, in this village – how extraordinary!

A bottle of schnapps was brought, and everyone had a sip; and over there was the church where the young woman had been laid down all those years ago, and right beside it, just as it was supposed to, ran the road where his uncle's cart had stood.

Jonathan walked over to the church, a red-brick building with whitewashed transoms. It was a church that could easily have stood in Schleswig-Holstein or Mecklenburg ('Our fallen heroes'). He was approaching it from the back, and to reach it he had to scramble down a slippery, sloping bank. A stream trickled along the bottom, the kind children like to throw stones in, with a concrete slab across it for churchgoers to take a short cut.

As Jonathan was edging his way down the slope he slipped

and hit the back of his head. Brightness filled his brain like a ball of lightning.

For a moment he was dazed. Something had changed. For several seconds the terrific blow had shaped the thought and image particles of his brain into lines of sound and stars, indecipherable yet meaningful.

The numbness gradually wore off. No one had seen him, thank God; the others had gone round the front, as this route was too treacherous for them. Jonathan was ashamed that, at the age of forty-three, he had slipped and fallen.

If Winkelvoss had taken a tumble here, with all her scarves and necklaces and trinkets, it might have been amusing, Jonathan thought. He and Hansi Strohtmeyer would have had something to laugh about together for quite some time.

Jonathan teetered across the concrete slab, climbed up the small slope covered in nettles and found himself already standing in the church's little cemetery. Stretched out in front of him were fresh graves with wooden crosses, faded flowers and wreaths and headstones from the German days, the names chiselled out one letter at a time. Wild bushes – elder, hazel, jasmine and laburnum – grew along the tumbledown wall. Jonathan was quite alone. He stared at a spot on the wall and knew: that's where *she* lies. He was neither sad nor happy; he wasn't even surprised that he was standing here, in a graveyard; he was neither cold nor warm; there was a little sunshine, a little wind. He could have walked on, but instead he stood staring and listening as if mesmerized. He saw the humus-rich soil, the tendrils of ivy, a bumblebee flying back and forth; there were sparrows, an aeroplane, the voices of the others. He also saw before him – and this disturbed him – the picture he had seen hanging on the wall at the Kuschinskis', the mass-produced painting of the young mother lying in a meadow, lifting her child above her head.

When Frau Winkelvoss called from the road – Hello! Was he dreaming over there, or what? – he tore himself away and walked over to the rest of the group. They'd just seen something wonderful, she said; they'd opened the church door, and a teacher had been sitting in the vestibule with a few dear little children ('mites', she called them) preparing for their First Communion. On old benches, just like a hundred years ago.

So children now sat in the vestibule where his mother had been set down back then, beside the board with the black numbers for the hymnal. Jonathan felt no need to see this. What would he have said to the children? Guess what: many, many years ago, this is what happened here?

Here, then, is where she breathed her last, he thought; and he didn't mind when Anita Winkelvoss grabbed his forearm and gave it a sympathetic squeeze.

Jonathan walked back to the car. A kind of numbness had taken possession of him. He couldn't muster any strong feeling that might have enabled him outwardly to express what had happened here. He felt detached yet completely focused; he was outside himself yet fully present.

Hansi Strohtmeyer was standing by the car, watching him. As he was about to get in, this man, who had driven in a rally across the Sahara and been stranded in a river in South America, asked him, 'What about your father?' Only then did Jonathan start to sob. He clutched his head and just managed to flee into the car; he saw before him a young lieutenant in riding breeches, a Wehrmacht lieutenant with a silver Wound Badge. He saw him standing on the shore of the Vistula Spit, scanning the sea with his binoculars – 'When are they going to come and get us?' – while behind him the refugee wagons rumbled from east to west and west to east. Jonathan pounded the armrest with his fist and the words kept hammering in his brain: all for nothing! ALL FOR NOTHING! He didn't mean the death of his mother or of his father, who'd had to 'bite the dust', or the sofa beds his uncle manufactured, but the suffering of all creatures, the flesh lashed to the stake, the calf he had seen bound and gagged, the torture chamber in the Marienburg, the shuffling procession of mankind beneath the condemning sky.

It's all for nothing, he thought, again and again. And: Who's to blame?

17

As they continued their journey they picked over all that had happened: how nice the old farmer had been; barely a tooth in his head, and they hadn't actually understood what it was he wanted, but he had been awfully nice. And all the others were nice as well, said Frau Winkelvoss; in time of need, if ever the shoe were on the other foot, she could imagine sticking it out with them.

'. . . for about half an hour,' Hansi Strohtmeyer added, but was ignored.

The business with the apples was awfully nice of them too; they hadn't needed to do that. And that hiding place. What if they'd probed a bit longer? No? They could have got some more details out of them for sure. All the other stuff that must still be waiting to be discovered – buried treasures! They'll stumble across them in five hundred years, like pots of gold coins from the Thirty Years War.

The graveyard business had really affected him, hadn't it? asked Frau Winkelvoss. She'd seen him standing there like that and thought: Why's he standing there? And then she'd known: I have to speak to him right away or something will happen. What she would really have liked to have done was to take a photo of him. That would have been a nice memory.

*

And the children in the church, sitting there, so well-behaved. Frau Winkelvoss, who was a Catholic, told them a curate had boxed her ears once and she hadn't been back to church since.

When she had finished recounting this experience, she shared the next chapter of her adoption narrative, alternating the story with the route book – 'After five kilometres, turn left. Watch out for horse-drawn vehicles.' Initially, she'd wanted to fly out on her own, to Brazil, but she'd never have got through it without her husband. All that *baksheesh*, slipping hundred-dollar notes into the hands of every judge and every lawyer. The whole enterprise had taken her eight days. Six adults in a Fiat Uno, forty-five degrees in the shade! Ninety-eight per cent humidity, car doors locked, windows up! Gravel roads, huge mud holes. And the people. It was like driving through an anthill of poverty; people living in their own filth.

And then, after a five-hour drive, the orphanage: an iron gate, two honks of the horn, a solitary, disabled black man in the yard, and suddenly the door of the orphanage opened and the children overwhelmed her like a hundred thousand flies, all of them black; they knew perfectly well that when white people came they took some of them away with them. And then an ancient woman had appeared, the founder of the home – 'They're just fetching her, the girl. Three months old; we found her on a step.' Then the child had been placed in her arms, and it had been harder than giving birth to a child of her own. A combination of excitement and bacteria had given her the shits.

Then back to the authorities: photographs, passport office, welfare office, court all over again.

*

Jonathan sat in his corner and saw in his mind's eye a beach, summer, heard the distant sounds of people bathing. And he saw his elegant father on horseback in the dunes, rising in the saddle, gazing off at the horizon. He would be around seventy now if he'd survived – quite conceivable – his mother sixty-five. Jonathan wished he were back on Isestrasse in Hamburg. What was he doing driving around this region? Isestrasse: easy street, breezy street, sleazy street. He didn't wish he was with Ulla. It was the thought of the quiet room, the Botero hanging on the wall, the washbasin, in front of which he could watch the schoolchildren throwing their sandwiches to the ducks during break, and the thought of his work that filled him with voluptuous satisfaction. The northern goddesses . . . Perhaps he should go to Flanders, or possibly Sweden?

Ulla Bakkre de Vaera – what had she been getting up to these past few days? What did she 'get up to', as a rule? What did she do? He remembered Langeoog, where he'd met her in the island bookshop one morning as he was about to buy his newspapers. She'd mistaken him for a member of staff, and he hadn't disabused her. A black blouse with silver embroidery, and black silk shorts, the seams split open a centimetre up the sides. Did he have the diaries of Novalis? she'd asked. Novalis, on Langeoog, in the island bookshop! And they'd gone to the cafe together, laughing, as if that had always been their intention, even though they didn't know each other at all. And at night, on the cool beach . . . He'd liked her cynicism, the way she talked about people without inhibition, with a friendly smile, and the way she had taken possession of him right from the start.

*

The car purred on. Hansi Strohtmeyer was delighted by the homeland association's West German omnibus, which was driving ahead of them, bouncing slightly; it was from Düsseldorf, a superbus with air conditioning and a toilet, a superbus with extra leg room. The trees lining the road waved their crowns in the wind; there was no hope whatsoever of overtaking it.

After an hour the bus turned off to the left, exactly where the Santubara crew wanted to turn as well. A narrow road led into the pine forest, and they came to a sign: BYŁA WOJENNA KWATERA HITLERA – the Wolf's Lair, Hitler's headquarters.

The Magirus-Deutz bus slid noiselessly into the car park, and before all the one-eyed, one-legged and one-armed gentlemen with their red-cheeked spouses could spill out of it, Hansi Strohtmeyer drove past and parked in a special parking space alongside a campervan, from which a dark-haired woman stared out.

You couldn't see much from the car park apart from the huge, half-demolished bunker by the entrance. The Führer's headquarters! From behind a high wire fence steel rods curved out of the yawning cracks. It was a bit like the zoo, where before you went in you might, with a bit of luck, spot a bear on imitation rocks and hear parrots screeching in the distance.

There was a booth with a hole in the glass for entry tickets – NO PHOTOGRAPHY! – and a board beside it with explanatory texts in five languages. No. 13 is Hitler's bunker, Bunker 16 is Göring, 19 Keitel. No. 15 isn't a bunker at all; that was a tea-room, and there was a casino here too. The homeland association's tour guide informed the Polish cashier that they all deeply regretted the fact that Germans had done so many dreadful things to her motherland, and he needed a group ticket for thirty-six adults and three children; did that qualify for a discount?

Hansi Strohtmeyer was fretting about the campervan; it didn't fill him with confidence. He wondered whether he should go back again and park the car elsewhere?

No need. Their escort commando's yellow Lada had already shown up and was parking on the edge of the forest. Herr Schütte was keeping a watchful eye on their precious V8.

Jonathan thought about Claus von Stauffenberg, hero and traitor, Hitler's failed assassin. He tried to imagine how he must have felt, arriving here with his little pistol on his belt, the heavy briefcase under his arm. The escape may have required even more careful planning than the attack. Tick-tick-tick, the clock against the table leg. Exiting the barracks again without anyone noticing. Using carefully fabricated excuses to get out of there, passing through the security zones, faster and faster, one after another . . . And then his reception in Berlin – all is lost – and instead of shaking his hand and thanking him they put him up against the wall.

Jonathan also wondered whether his father might ever have had business here; and Stauffenberg's face superimposed itself on his father's, and he thought: If he had to die anyway, why didn't he just gun Hitler down then and there?

Frau Winkelvoss hesitated a moment before entering. She probably thought visiting this curious site was more of a men's thing. Two scruffy men who clearly belonged to the campervan snuck past, eyeing her insolently. The woman in the campervan shouted something at them before they could hassle her, though, and it was all right. Frau Winkelvoss regarded Jonathan – his slim, intellectual build, the wonky, spotted bow-tie – and thought of the hour they'd spent beside the lake, and suddenly it struck her that she hadn't really tried to get to know this person at all yet. She'd always talked to Strohtmeyer, whom she knew anyway, instead of linking arms with this eccentric man who was at home in editorial departments and had been to America at a time when no one had been to America.

As Jonathan prepared to enter the mossy, grass-covered iconic site – notebook in hand, ready to write up his impressions, perhaps even to find an unusual angle – she pushed her way over to him and started talking. Did he really think, she asked him, that the rally journalists would be interested in this Nazi crap? Wouldn't it be better to leave it out because it would stir up the wrong emotions? All they were really meant to be doing was test-driving the new V8s; what did that have to do with Hitler's bunker? And then – God alone knows why – she treated Jonathan to a promotional lecture on Sicily, where there were also ruins to be visited, because whenever the country had been overrun by another new culture the pre-existing one had been wiped out and the people exterminated.

Liszt's Préludes sounded faintly in Jonathan's head; he saw that officer on horseback on the Champs-Élysées, waving a greeting to the German soldiers as they marched past the Arc de Triomphe. Frau Winkelvoss went on talking. She spoke of unbelievable heat, and Stromboli, 926 metres high and still active. Jonathan found himself thinking about that stooped, doddering man walking up and down here with his German shepherd, the man who had managed to get multitudes of people to slit each other's throats with bloody knives. A photo he had once seen pushed itself to the front of his mind: winter '41, three ordinary soldiers lost in a snowstorm and whipping their horse as it tried, beneath their blows, to leap out of a snowdrift. Meanwhile Frau Winkelvoss was praising Sicily's natural beauty, the flat, undulating landscape; he must go there in spring when it was carpeted with flowers, although the people had cut down all the trees.

Frau Winkelvoss talked and talked, then suddenly woke up to the fact that Jonathan wasn't speaking. Was he still upset about the business with his mother? she asked. She'd seen him standing there, rooted to the spot, and she'd thought: You have to call out to him now or something will happen. She'd sensed that something unusual was going on.

They walked into the black canyon of trees and a light rain began to fall. NO MORE WAR! Big admonishing signs to the right and left of the path summoned visitors to a didactic audio-visual presentation, but Jonathan skipped the lecture. He was looking for the original experience – he wanted to touch, feel, inhale the relics of the Third Reich; he was fed up with photos and newsreel footage.

He took a photocopy of the site map out of his wallet – thank God he'd picked the thing up, that way he wouldn't confuse Himmler's bunker with Göring's. And already they were there: concrete cubes to the left and right of the path, with concrete roofs fifteen metres thick, their corners worn away, draped in moss-furred camouflage netting with artificial foliage on top.

Hansi Strohtmeyer elbowed his way over, curious. He did, after all, want to know which bunker had belonged to whom, and the measurements, so-and-so many metres high, wide and deep. The fact that beneath the surface layer of concrete, in the ground, there were another six floors where everything was probably still intact: desks, bunk beds, filing cabinets. Nobody dared to go down there because there were thought to be glass-mines buried in the earth.

The bunkers had been blown up with many wagon-loads of dynamite, but that had only scratched the surface.

Strohtmeyer wondered whether perhaps speleologists could take a look down there. Venture into the depths with a red rope around their waists to find skeletons in uniform slumped over a field telephone.

After Jonathan had answered his colleague, he was forced to let Frau Winkelvoss lecture him about Sicily some more. The train that circumnavigated Etna resembled an iron sausage; and the rumbling in the volcano's interior, the puffing and growling . . .

Soft, gentle rain dripping from the branches of the trees on to the bunkers, streaming down the walls. Rampant nature, damp now and gleaming; the mosses on the walls of the concrete blocks, the earthen track through the forest, the silence over all: this had to be inhaled through flared nostrils. Jonathan saw the bunkers as standing stones; among them, in the last days of humanity, in the red of the setting sun, the last survivors were gathering.

What must Poles think when they walked around this place? said Frau Winkelvoss. Did they regularly bring schoolchildren here? It was the best history lesson you could come up with.

Strohtmeyer said it was strange: if Hitler had been so sure of himself, why did he build these bunkers? The man who invented the blitzkrieg, of all people, hiding away in these concrete monstrosities. He could have survived a nuclear bomb in there.

Yes, that really was odd. Jonathan was surprised he hadn't thought of it himself. He decided to write it down and use it in his article. And then, of course, to highlight the parallels with the Marienburg. He'd quote Scharnhorst – what was it again? Anyone who barricades themselves in has already lost?

Göring's bunker, Jodl's bunker, Keitel's bunker – they almost walked right past the historic spot where the bomb went off. There wasn't much left of the barracks where Hitler, in steel-rimmed glasses, had held his briefings; you could still make out the foundations. Jonathan thought of the photos of Hitler's valet showing journalists the Führer's tattered trousers, a general's bandaged head, and the photo of Mussolini – Hitler picking him up from the station, telling him how lucky he'd just been, again, it had been Providence, and so forth. Bormann in the background, triumphant.

Not far away: Hitler's bunker. Fifteen tons of dynamite hadn't managed to get the better of it – it had only listed slightly to one side, and thus it stood and would still be standing in a thousand years.

A Polish boy ran up and beckoned to them: here, there was a hidden entrance around the back, he could lead them in, no one had ever been inside. None of the three had any enthusiasm for a dangerous tour of discovery.

Jonathan photographed a few more curiosities. Graffiti – HITLER KAPUT! – and a few thin branches, propped up against the sloping concrete wall of a demolished bunker, as if forestalling its collapse. A school class must have arranged them at an art teacher's behest: a joke, to show that mankind will always transcend history and may even do so with a light heart.

Jonathan found it amusing that a state-owned plastic waste-paper basket had been installed right next to Hitler's bunker.

Jonathan pocketed a lump of wall: he would take it home for his girlfriend, Ulla. A shame that the famous film Hitler had made of the conspirators' strangulation was no longer extant. This document as part of the cruelty exhibition, showing non-stop on a loop in a black-curtained cabinet, for an additional admission fee? After all, the cameramen must have applied the aesthetic rules of their work in this film too: close-up, pan and zoom.

The rain had stopped. They were almost at the exit when the omnibus fellowship came walking towards them, the ladies and gentlemen they had already encountered at the Marienburg and in Sensburg. Invigorated by the audio-visual presentation, they were now excited to be inspecting this place to which, back in the glory days, they would not have been granted access.

The car was still there. The two Poles had joined the woman in the campervan; they could be heard laughing, and shortly afterwards the vehicle started rocking rhythmically from side to side.

Outside, the bus driver had sat down on a bench with a vacuum flask and some cheese sandwiches. Hansi Strohtmeyer asked if he might take a look at the driver's cab. He was even allowed to turn on the engine and drive a couple of metres forward and back, he who had roared across African deserts and been stranded in a South American river. This experience far surpassed the viewing of stacks of concrete. Quick, though, switch it off again – it would not be good if a *militsiya* man came along and asked to see his driving licence.

When they finally drove off, Jonathan thought he saw his father standing in the entrance to one of the bunkers. Had he taken shelter there? How much longer would this go on?

18

Late that evening they got back to Danzig, which already felt familiar to them somehow – 'all those dear little alleyways', as Anita Winkelvoss put it. The tourism general was waiting for them because of the stolen car; he was dreadfully sorry, he said, the whole thing was a terrible embarrassment for him. His motherland had suffered a blow to its reputation; but it was one eight-cylinder car the richer, just as it would be the richer for the twenty-six journalists who would soon be driving along its shaded country roads (which belonged to Poland, now and for ever) and spending lots of money.

There was news of Herr Schmidt, the sophisticated gourmet: alas, he couldn't come at all now. Wasn't that just typical! Mess up all the arrangements, then make yourself scarce. Had Jonathan, perhaps, made any notes about the menus?

Walking up the steps to the Pod Łososiem restaurant, they felt like extras in the nostalgic film *The Punch Bowl*. The atmosphere was dignified, with music from a band calling itself 'Hot Chocolades'. A beggar who tried to follow them with an outstretched hand was turned away by the doorman.

Bread soup with sausage, a portion of eel or fillet of zander – that was the question. Hansi stuck to *piwo* and Anita

Winkelvoss to a yellow *likier*, namely Bananowy Havana Club at one hundred and fifty zlotys a glass. Once again she informed the baffled waiter that the dry wine was too sweet for her. Tomorrow they would be home! That put her in a good mood.

Jonathan didn't stay for the end of the farewell party; he left to chase his phantom. That knee, sticking out from under the blanket: a sign, surely? 'Come again'?

But he couldn't find the slip of paper on which he had noted the street; it had gone missing when the car was stolen. He wandered up and down the alleyways like an Italian tenor singing, 'Maria, carissima Maria!' But he failed to find the house. The alleyways made him feel even more as if he had strayed into a film, with the full moon and a steamer honking in the distance, and his adventurous spirit dissipated.

What a pity, Jonathan thought as he got into bed. I really could have helped those people.

And he went through all the things he could have sent them; and then he would have brought them to Germany and sat in Blankenese with Maria, a mountain of ice cream with a little paper umbrella on top, feasting on her amazement at the ships slowly sailing down the Elbe, and they would have sat there so comfortably, eating their ice cream – she would never have experienced anything like it.

What would she think of him when the medicine didn't arrive? 'Typical Westerner,' they would say. 'Smug and selfish.'

After breakfast they got into an argument over whether they should drive on to Stutthof, a concentration camp that didn't appear in any encyclopaedia.

'Oh, no, that's taking things too far,' said Frau Winkelvoss, who had flown halfway round the world to get herself a child. She'd had a teacher who had talked incessantly, for years, about all that Jewish stuff, always showing those terrible pictures. That had been enough for her, thank you. And then she proceeded to talk about how the Germans had shot Jews in Poland and had even gone on to gas them in Auschwitz.

But Hansi Strohtmeyer stuck to his guns: although the camp wasn't directly on the route, they should at least 'offer' it to those who came on the rally. And to do that they had to drive there and check out the parking situation and whether you could go to the toilet or grab a snack. There were bound to be those journalists who would just be waiting for them to forget the concentration camp – and then they'd write in their newspapers that the Santubara Company with its automated vehicle-manufacturing plant was ignoring the Holocaust. No – he glanced at his black watch, which had two dials, was waterproof, and still showed the precise time even at a depth of thirty metres – he was going to drive to Stutthof now; she could stay in the hotel and settle up.

That was fine with Frau Winkelvoss. She took her shoes off under the table, lit a cigarette and ordered a 'citron natur', as she called it, for which she was given fizzy lemonade. She sorted through the amber jewellery she had bought on their trip, even though she didn't actually like amber, and watched the people from the homeland association crowd into the hotel shop to make a few last purchases. How extraordinary that they didn't have plates with coats of arms on here either!

The question now was whether Jonathan should go with Hansi. He was caught on the horns of a tricky dilemma: look for Maria or go to the concentration camp? He was inclined towards Maria, but he couldn't risk skipping the camp. Five thousand marks, negotiable? This was an opportunity to find a totally unexpected angle for his article. There was no getting out of Stutthof.

It was already nine o'clock – high time to get going, as they were supposed to return home that afternoon. So off they drove in their freshly washed vehicle – which, strangely, had been scratched by a nail all along its side. The technicians in their grey outfits waved to them, and this time Jonathan sat in front. Hansi Strohtmeyer set the route book aside; the road led straight on, pot-holes or no, and even a journalist who didn't have the first idea about driving could figure that one out if he needed to.

They didn't talk much. Whatever awaited them wasn't going to be a picnic.

They passed through places that had once had very curious names, as Jonathan could see from his old map: 'Haystall' and 'Beansack', 'New World' and 'Squirefield'. They drove over a green-painted swing bridge, then had to take a ferry across the Weichsel. A Düsseldorf-registered Mercedes with tinted windows was already on board; a man and a woman, in tinted spectacles, elderly people dressed in pale grey and white who knew that this was a ferry from the German era and informed each other of this fact so loudly that everyone was forced to hear. The Poles couldn't even manage to construct a new ferry!

Jonathan had looked it up. This Weichsel crossing had been a bottleneck in those January days in 1945. This was where the Wehrmacht's wood-gas cars had given their all and farmers had whipped their horses. And this was where British bombers had carried out their mission to finish off the remaining refugees, people already under fire from Red Army tanks as they tried to escape to the opposite bank with their chests of drawers and their grandfather clocks. The gentlemen had sat in the cockpits in their smart leather outfits, smoking Craven 'A' cigarettes, nice and warm and dry, Dunkirk still fresh in their minds. They'd pointed down below: how many bombs have we got left? Come on, let's fly over one last time and show the rabble down there what comes of voting for a criminal like Hitler. Ninety-eight per cent for Germany? Here you go. And the best of it was, they didn't even hit the ferry.

Hansi Strohtmeyer took the route book and made an entry saying that although there was no bridge here a ferry shuttled back and forth, and there was no need to get annoyed if it was just setting off when you rushed up, drenched in sweat, because it would come straight back again – if it was running, that is.

The Vistula Spit. Ah, the curved lines of spume foaming incessantly towards the shore, the storm-tattered pines. The things they could do with tourism here, said Hansi Strohtmeyer – they could be raking it in without even getting their hands dirty. Forget about the shipyard in Danzig. Cafes, hotels, restaurants, horses for hire to gallop along the beach . . . And he made some notes about where you might build such a hotel, and (more quietly) started totting up his savings to see whether he had enough to do it someday.

Jonathan had thought the spit was at least ten kilometres wide; that was what it looked like on the map. Now he saw that it was just a single road with a strip of land on either side. And here, on this narrow spit, the refugees had trotted up and down after the death march over the frozen lagoon, all escape routes blocked. They hadn't been able to get through to Danzig or Pillau. And so they stood packed together, day after day, night after night, staring up at the sky.

In Stutthof they had a pleasant surprise, as Hansi Strohtmeyer put it: the concentration camp was shut. A sign on the door said CLOSED TODAY, which was something of a godsend, they both thought. No need to look around these barracks and the torture bench in the museum as well and then be picked on by the museum guide because, as Germans, they were responsible for the deaths of hundreds of thousands of Hungarian Jews.

Hansi Strohtmeyer rattled the gate and squinted through the bars. Nothing to be done about it. He was peering into the compound the way people back then must have yearned to get out.

The Düsseldorf Mercedes with the tinted windows pulled up nearby, and the man and woman got out. God knows what they were doing here. Perhaps the man had been with the SS and had ridden along the beach back then, with the prisoners doffing their caps.

No, the situation was quite different. The woman was the focus here. She'd been a prisoner and had worked in the laundry; that was how she'd escaped with her life. They'd made the long trip specially, she told Hansi Strohtmeyer, from Connecticut to Germany. Couldn't they, between them, persuade the camp to make an exception? She talked and talked while the man circled the Japanese Santubara car, inspecting it with a disagreeable expression. He traced the tip of his finger along the scratch.

'No, it's closed today,' said a Pole who came shuffling up the path. A *delegacja* from Hungary had wanted to survey the remains of the camp in peace and quiet, so they couldn't visit or make notes about anything. Five marks didn't get them anywhere either. He had a few German banknotes, the Pole said: they looked very odd to him; were they still legal tender? No, they weren't; they were so-called 'Rentenmarks', issued in 1934, and could be thrown away with a clear conscience; not even a homeland museum would take them. The couple in their tinted Mercedes couldn't have helped either. They had already driven off.

When the man realized there was nothing he could do with the money – that he'd been conned – he uttered a quite disgusting curse, which they could only assume was directed at them. There was nothing to be done.

'You know what?' said Hansi Strohtmeyer. 'If we can't get in here, at least let's drive to your father.'

Jonathan responded firmly in the negative. He couldn't ask that of him; and why rake up all the old stories? Anyway, wasn't it far too late already? Would they still make the flight?

A bunker overlooking the water, right by Kahlberg; that was what he'd been told. A single bomb: 'Your father knew nothing about it, he died instantly . . .' And Jonathan didn't want to go there, but he had no say in the matter. Hansi Strohtmeyer wouldn't be talked out of his idea, which had come to him the previous night. He turned the big car around, and they slowly drew closer. God knows, it wasn't far. These few extra kilometres wouldn't make any difference; the excess barely registered on the test vehicle's digital display. And whereas before he had been almost silent, Hansi Strohtmeyer now started talking in detail about races in which he had taken part. It had been in Africa that he'd heard of a black farmer who had planted nothing but melons in the year of the rally because he'd thought the racing drivers and journalists passing through his village would be eager for refreshment. The man had put all his money and a year's work into the melon field, had set out his tables – and then? Whoosh-whoosh-whoosh, and it was all over. Half an hour of thundering, not a single melon sold.

In Krynica Morska, or Kahlberg, there were a few pretty little houses with green-painted verandas facing the street and gladioli next to the fence. Germans had lived here once, ordinary people; they were little German houses with German verandas, painted green. Perhaps the corner house had been the commandant's office, where wireless operators had sat at drop-leaf tables receiving the final orders. Perhaps a German lieutenant had sat there, wondering whether he still had any chance of getting away.

It wasn't hard to get their bearings. At the crossroads they turned left down to the water. They could already hear and smell the Baltic Sea. Hansi Strohtmeyer used to zip across it in a speedboat if he happened to have time between one race and the next. Jonathan had no memories of the Baltic. When he was a child he and his uncle used to go to the North Sea, year after year, to Langeoog, with kite, bucket and spade. Then, years later, he had met Ulla Bakkre de Vaera there, early one morning at the bookshop where he'd gone to buy his newspapers. She had been the one who initiated their relationship; and those had been good times, so unaccustomed and easy. He thought of his girlfriend's black shorts with their split side-seams, but they aroused no feelings in him.

The only constant in life is chance, thought Jonathan.

Yellow- and blue-painted fishing boats lay on the beach; men were loading them up with nets. Their ultrasound had registered a few fish swimming twenty degrees north-northwest. The fishes' gills would catch in the nets; small and big fish would be plucked out, bellies slit, guts removed, and the pretty ladies in spotless fish shops would want their fillet fresh, and they'd be fried up in butter.

Hansi Strohtmeyer let Jonathan walk ahead of him like a diviner; he kept a close eye on him to make sure he didn't break off and say something like, 'This is pointless, you know.' They hadn't made this detour for him to do that. Hansi Strohtmeyer wasn't assuming Jonathan knew the exact location of the bunker his father had been sitting in when it occurred to him to step out into the night: smoke a cigarette, flick the lighter and it was all over. He was following Jonathan to make him go on searching. Surely instinct would lead him to the spot where his father had perished.

Jonathan really didn't know where it was. He heard the water and the seagulls, saw the fishermen. He'd never listened properly when he was told: a bunker in the dunes, right at the water's edge, that's where your father was killed. What had been more interesting was that there hadn't been much of him left: they'd picked up the silver Wound Badge, and a shoe lying in the marram grass.

Jonathan forced himself to think of the Wehrmacht lieutenant who was his father: field cap with fold, breeches. A stranger, yet so close, still here – here again. A hard, unshaven cheek against his cheek, and the suitcase full of diaries and letters in Uncle Edwin's attic in Bad Zwischenahn, unopened to this day. His father was a dead man who sensed that, right here and now, someone was gathering up his final seconds on this earth; a dead man who rose now out of the warm mud where he had lain, had slept for so long. A soul now looking across to see: was it *him* they meant? Or was it, perhaps, a mistake? What was his connection with the young man down there, hair blown forward by the wind, now striding up to the spot where it had happened all those years ago, where the lightning flash had torn off his head and atomized his limbs.

Jonathan was prepared to shout, 'It was here!' just to put an end to the traipsing through the sand, but that wouldn't have worked; Hansi Strohtmeyer wouldn't have accepted it. He was growing more watchful by the minute. He wanted to know, precisely.

It was a beautiful day. Jonathan gazed out across the smooth, swelling water to a horizon veiled in mist. On a wooden terrace, which must once have been a cafe with a dance floor, some soldiers were keeping watch, looking through their binoculars to see what the young man was doing down there in his spotted bow-tie, a small vertical figure in this wide-open landscape.

Jonathan turned away and looked up at the dunes. That was when he noticed a radio antenna. He took a few clumsy steps across the soft Baltic sand and saw that it belonged to a military observation post, a barracks, and in front of it lay the ruins of a small bunker. Jonathan indicated to Hansi Strohtmeyer: there it is. They got to within twenty paces before they were shouted at by the soldiers on guard, whose task it was to ensure that no one approached the sacred motherland from the sea. What were they doing here? the soldiers shouted. Hansi Strohtmeyer took it upon himself to answer: they'd thought this was an ice cream stall; it was very hot today. And Jonathan stood with his back to the bunker, and saw now what his father had seen in his final hours. He looked all the way out to the plumes of smoke on the horizon, and if this look had been a physical thing, a dove perhaps, it could have returned as an echo. In that moment, every look ever sent out from this spot could have returned: his father's gaze, searching through his binoculars – were the transport ships coming soon? – Denmark! – the refugees' looks of hope, the desperation of the Jews – and the nonchalance of the pre-war ladies slathering themselves with Nivea and watching sailing boats tilt to the side. All that nonchalance would have returned on the wind, all those hopes, all that despair, as a gust of faded images.

Jonathan bent down, scooped up a little sand and poured it into Maria's medicine bottle. Perhaps a forensic institute could have identified microscopic fragments of his father among the tiny brown, black and quartz pebbles. And that was the end of the ceremony. Hansi Strohtmeyer shouted, 'Bye, then!' to the soldiers. The fishermen bent over their boats, the birds flew away and the Wehrmacht lieutenant sank back into the warm mud from which he had been summoned.

'It was my son, looking for me,' he whispered to his comrades. And they passed the message on: 'His son was looking for him.'

And Jonathan thought: My mother breathed her last during the evacuation, and my father was killed on the Vistula Spit.

I have called thee by thy name; thou art mine.

19

Late that afternoon the LOT aeroplane landed in Hamburg. The colourful line of passengers emerging from it included Jonathan Fabrizius, his impractical but sturdy holdall bumping the backs of his knees. He was carrying his coat over his arm and Memling's *The Last Judgement* rolled up in his hand, a little gift for Ulla: the damned tumbling into hell, the bland blessed ascending to God. Jonathan was preoccupied: the trip had been more of a strain than he had anticipated. This boded well for the reunion with his girlfriend. She would look at him and say, 'Darling, you look exhausted!' And then they'd have a fry-up, and he would tell her what had happened to him on the trip. She would simply listen, and then, in the night, there would be a whistle.

On the concourse, overlaid by announcements for passengers heading to Tenerife to take advantage of the off-season to swim, eat and sleep, the puffy-bloused Frau Winkelvoss, who was thirty-eight years old, gave Jonathan her card and said he should call her if ever he found himself in Frankfurt; she had a guest room with its own toilet; he could stay over any time; her husband would be delighted. She called him 'Joe'. Then she gave him a kiss on the cheek. She would return home to her husband and child, a husband who sported a comb-over and a child who was called names like 'café au lait' on the street.

Hansi Strohtmeyer, the 'chauffeur' with nerves of steel, shook Jonathan's hand, squeezing so hard that the latter went weak at the knees. He looked at the man again and hesitated.

This was an interlude, he thought. People like this are ten a penny . . . 'There's no point,' he said quietly, and set off for Eppendorf in a taxi with a pop song playing:

Oh, oh, oh, in Mexico,
Where the boys are glad to go,
'Cause in every jungle town
There are girls both black and brown
Shaking their booties to and fro . . .

For a moment Jonathan wondered whether he ought to look in on Albert Schindeloe, tell him that life in West Germany was enough to make you puke and they should go to East Prussia together sometime soon; that once you'd been to East Prussia it really had a hold over you; those magnificent avenues – from German times! – the endearingly disorganized Poles . . . Jonathan knew for certain that he would never go back. Florence, the Gates of Paradise or Castel del Monte – that would be something quite different from the fearful brickwork of the Marienburg. Or Flanders perhaps, in search of northern goddesses.

He didn't go to see Schindeloe; instead, he asked to be dropped off at Isestrasse 13. He rushed up the stairs as he always did, overtaking the juddering lift in which the general's widow was going up, taking refuge in the apartment just before her.

And then came the big surprise: it was empty. Not his own room, of course, but his girlfriend's. Ulla Bakkre de Vaera had cleared out, right down to the cotton wool in the bathroom. She had taken advantage of his absence to go and join her boss. The attic apartment on the top floor of the museum had convinced her. Three rooms, wallpapered in the colours of the Frauenplan, and a sweet little tiny bathroom. Her belongings had been brought over in the museum van, and Dr Kranstöver had pressed a bunch of gladioli into her hands. He had brought round, in person, a painting from the museum's collection: a Danish painting of a girl in a bobble hat. At this very moment Ulla Bakkre de Vaera was sure to be found hanging paintings in the museum – a descent from the Cross, perhaps – while Dr Kranstöver, in his office, placed a silver-framed photo of an older woman in his desk drawer and slipped some banknotes into his wallet. Drive to France for a few days, relax before the fuss of the exhibition began, with a person at his side whose mysteries he was eager to explore. She would hand him a cup of bitter tea as lizards darted across the slate chippings. Perhaps Fortune would smile on him and give him a few more golden moments. Time was not on his side.

Ulla's room was empty, and Jonathan didn't understand it. This was where she had lived, played patience and listened to the Piano Concerto in E-flat major, and now she was gone. Jonathan opened the sliding door that had always been blocked by Ulla's bookshelves; he strolled across to his room, to his leather sofa and kitchen table, and back again to Ulla's window, where the kitsch vases had sat upon the ledge. A train rattled past on the elevated railway.

There was no doubt about it: Ulla had left him, taking with

her the Callot etching of the person being quartered and the Gallé lamp that had shed such a cosy light on the table as her delicate hands rearranged the cards in her index of cruelty. She had packed up and moved away, presumably with the help of Albert Schindeloe. Jonathan was sure he would be able to read the lawyerish reasons for her sudden disappearance in the letter propped on the window ledge. And all the reasons would be reasonable, and he still wouldn't understand them.

Whom was he to tell now about his East Prussian days? About his experience of the past, and that it could be dangerous to delve into things that were better left alone? About the northern goddess in Danzig and its counterpart, the Marienburg? Which ultimately, on reflection, left him unsatisfied. All those utilitarian extensions . . . no, the Castel del Monte was far more compelling.

Jonathan went back to his room and set his bag on the table. He took out his notes and placed them beside the typewriter, then, still standing, typed a few letters on the old machine the way you tap on a piano at a friend's house – E, F-sharp, G-sharp, B, C – and your friends say, He's sad.

The E jammed, as it always did.

He thought of Rosenau and the graveyard wall and of how he had fallen over, the bright blow to the back of his head, and he saw an endless succession of doors very gradually closing.

'No matter,' he said aloud.

The bright, sunny room at the front of the house . . . He'd be able to move, put the table in front of the window. Yes, he thought, the best thing would be if he kept both rooms, then he could walk up and down, look out both front and back and put even more books on the floor. What a good thing he had made friends with the general's widow; she would agree to it. She was probably standing in the kitchen now, leaning over the sink to rid herself of her smoker's phlegm. Or was she pressing her ear to the wall and listening, to see whether he was taking it well or going to pieces at this stroke of fate?

'Croak.' The word came to him suddenly, and he knew who he meant by it, and he tried in vain to suppress the word. It referred to his uncle, who looked like Julius Streicher and yet was such a good man. Eighty-six years old? He would croak soon, you could be sure of that, and renting two rooms would be no problem then.

Strange that the Botero had been taken off the wall. The painting stood on the floor; the nail had been ripped out, the hole filled in.

What was that supposed to mean?

TRANSLATOR'S NOTE

The history of East Prussia is long and complex. Over the centuries the region has repeatedly changed hands, and under its various rulers its towns, villages, castles, churches and geographical features have been known by different names. Many Germans still use the familiar Teutonic ones – Danzig, for example, rather than Gdańsk. In German this does not have political overtones. It would, however, if someone were to use the new place names briefly imposed under the Nazis, as indicated on page 83 ('Gotenhafen').

The translator is faced with a conundrum. If no specific English name exists, which name should be used? Does one follow the original text and retain the German name? But what if in 1988, when the novel is set, this place was part of Poland, Lithuania or Russia? The choice of language has political and cultural implications. In the novel, for example, the driver, Hansi Strohtmeyer, makes a point of using Polish place names even when his colleagues do not.

The translator's decision is further complicated by the fact that the book refers to certain places at different periods in East Prussian history. Despite the usual preference for consistency, it would make no sense to use the Polish name of a village if the context is that of a predominantly German settlement in the Third Reich.

The story is told primarily from the point of view of Jonathan Fabrizius, whose ambivalent relationship with his East Prussian homeland is at the heart of the novel. Jonathan takes pride in the region's German history. He hunts down an old map with German place names and often expresses irritation with the Polish ones. I have therefore, for the most part, adhered to Jonathan's perspective by retaining the German names; but I have used Polish or Lithuanian names where these are specified in the original, and when quoting characters whose perspective is not a German one. In this translation, for example, the Polish tour guide at Malbork Castle refers to the Lithuanian leader as Vytautas, not Witold. (For Jonathan, of course, Malbork will always be Marienburg, the great fortress of the medieval Teutonic Order.)

The *Frische Nehrung*, *Frisches Haff*, *Kurische Nehrung* and *Kurisches Haff* are known in English as the Vistula Spit, Vistula Lagoon, Curonian Spit and Curonian Lagoon. I have used the English designations because the reader needs to be able to visualize them, but it is probably useful to know that Jonathan refers to the River Vistula – which empties into the Vistula Lagoon – by its German name, the Weichsel (Polish: Wisła).

Finally, the italicized quotations throughout the text of the book are from a wide variety of sources, including adaptations of works by German poets such as J. W. von Goethe and Agnes Miegel, as well as folk songs, patriotic songs, popular songs and verses of the twentieth century, and the chorale of Bach's *St Matthew Passion*.

Charlotte Collins
London, May 2018

GLOSSARY

German	Contemporary
Allenstein	POL: Olsztyn
Braunsberg	POL: Braniewo
Brodsack	POL: Chlebówka
Christburg	POL: Dzierzgoń
Danzig	POL: Gdańsk
Frauenburg	POL: Frombork
Gumbinnen	RUS: Gusev
Gdingen (NS: Gotenhafen)	POL: Gdynia
Heilsberg	POL: Lidzbark Warmiński
Kahlberg	POL: Krynica Morska
Kolberg	POL: Kołobrzeg
Krakau	POL: Kraków
Lodz	POL: Łódź
Masovia	POL: Mazowswe
Marienau	POL: Marynowy
Marienburg	POL: Malbork
Memel	LIT: Klaipėda
Nidden	LIT: Nida
Pillau	RUS: Baltiysk
Preussisch Holland	POL: Pasłęk (ENG: Prussian Holland)

Rastenburg	POL: Kętrzyn
Sensburg	POL: Mrągowo
Stettin	POL: Szczecin
Tannenberg	POL: Stębark
Zopot	POL: Sopot
Jakobskirche (Allenstein)	ENG: Church of St Jacob Cathedral
Marienkirche (Danzig)	ENG: St Mary's Church
River Oder	POL: Odra
River Nogat	POL: Nogat
River Weichsel	POL: Wisła; ENG: Vistula
Frische Nehrung	ENG: Vistula Spit
Frisches Haff	ENG: Vistula Lagoon
Kurische Nehrung	ENG: Curonian Spit
Kurisches Haff	ENG: Curonian Lagoon
Witold (Grand Duke of Lithuania)	LIT: Vytautas
Borislaw III (Prince of Poland)	POL: Bolesław III
Konrad von Masowien	ENG: Konrad of Masovia
Jagiello (Grand Duke of Lithuania, King of Poland)	POL: Jagiełło; LIT: Jogaila

POL: Polish; LIT: Lithuanian; RUS: Russian; ENG: English; NS: National Socialist (Nazi)

OTHER NEW YORK REVIEW CLASSICS

For a complete list of titles, visit www.nyrb.com or write to:
Catalog Requests, NYRB, 435 Hudson Street, New York, NY 10014

J.R. ACKERLEY Hindoo Holiday*
J.R. ACKERLEY My Dog Tulip*
J.R. ACKERLEY My Father and Myself*
HENRY ADAMS The Jeffersonian Transformation
RENATA ADLER Pitch Dark*
RENATA ADLER Speedboat*
ROBERT AICKMAN Compulsory Games*
LEOPOLDO ALAS His Only Son *with* Doña Berta*
CÉLESTE ALBARET Monsieur Proust
DANTE ALIGHIERI The Inferno
KINGSLEY AMIS The Alteration*
KINGSLEY AMIS Girl, 20*
KINGSLEY AMIS The Green Man*
KINGSLEY AMIS Lucky Jim*
KINGSLEY AMIS The Old Devils*
KINGSLEY AMIS One Fat Englishman*
ROBERTO ARLT The Seven Madmen*
U.R. ANANTHAMURTHY Samskara: A Rite for a Dead Man*
IVO ANDRIĆ Omer Pasha Latas*
WILLIAM ATTAWAY Blood on the Forge
W.H. AUDEN (EDITOR) The Living Thoughts of Kierkegaard
W.H. AUDEN W. H. Auden's Book of Light Verse
ERICH AUERBACH Dante: Poet of the Secular World
EVE BABITZ Eve's Hollywood*
EVE BABITZ I Used to Be Charming: The Rest of Eve Babitz*
EVE BABITZ Slow Days, Fast Company: The World, the Flesh, and L.A.*
DOROTHY BAKER Cassandra at the Wedding*
DOROTHY BAKER Young Man with a Horn*
J.A. BAKER The Peregrine
S. JOSEPHINE BAKER Fighting for Life*
HONORÉ DE BALZAC The Human Comedy: Selected Stories*
HONORÉ DE BALZAC The Memoirs of Two Young Wives*
VICKI BAUM Grand Hotel*
SYBILLE BEDFORD A Favorite of the Gods *and* A Compass Error*
SYBILLE BEDFORD Jigsaw*
SYBILLE BEDFORD A Legacy*
SYBILLE BEDFORD A Visit to Don Otavio: A Mexican Journey*
MAX BEERBOHM The Prince of Minor Writers: The Selected Essays of Max Beerbohm*
STEPHEN BENATAR Wish Her Safe at Home*
FRANS G. BENGTSSON The Long Ships*
WALTER BENJAMIN The Storyteller Essays*
ALEXANDER BERKMAN Prison Memoirs of an Anarchist
GEORGES BERNANOS Mouchette
MIRON BIAŁOSZEWSKI A Memoir of the Warsaw Uprising*
INÈS CAGNATI Free Day*
ADOLFO BIOY CASARES The Invention of Morel
PAUL BLACKBURN (TRANSLATOR) Proensa*

* *Also available as an electronic book.*